D1526960

Hart of Noel

a bookstrings "noella"

CHAUTONA HAVIG

PUBLICATIONS

Fonts: Adorn Condensed, Albino Lovebird, Berton
Cover Illustration: Joshua Markey
Cover Design: Chautona Havig
Edited by: Haug Editing and TWE Editing

The events and people in this book, aside from any caveats that
may appear on the next page, are purely fictional, and any
resemblance to actual people is purely coincidental. I'd love to
meet them!

FICTION / CHRISTIAN / ROMANCE

Welcome to The Mosaic Collection

We are sisters, a beautiful mosaic united by the love of God through the blood of Christ.

Each month The Mosaic Collection releases one faith-based novel or anthology exploring our theme, Family by His Design, and sharing stories that feature diverse, God-designed families. All are contemporary stories ranging from mystery and women's fiction to comedic and literary fiction. We hope you'll join our Mosaic family as we explore together what truly defines a family.

If you're like us, loneliness and suffering have touched your life in ways you never imagined; but Dear One, while you may feel alone in your suffering—whatever it is—you are never alone!

Subscribe to *Grace & Glory*, the official newsletter of The Mosaic Collection, to receive monthly encouragement from Mosaic authors, as well as timely updates about events, new releases, and giveaways.

Learn more about The Mosaic Collection at:

www.mosaiccollectionbooks.com
Join our Reader Community, too!
www.facebook.com/groups/TheMosaicCollection
If you'd like to find out about monthly launch team opportunities, sign up at
www.mosaiccollectionbooks.com/launch-team

Dedication

Dedicated to the beautiful town of Noel, Missouri. I miss you even more than ever after writing this.

One

Scrubbing a hand over his jaw, Joshua Hart peered out his bedroom window and grinned. Clear blue skies—not even one fluffy white cloud to mar them. There may be a storm coming near the end of the week, but Thanksgiving week had rolled into southwest Missouri like March's oft-touted lamb. Sure, it might be a bit brisk, but with the sun shining, it'd be above fifty in no time. It could reach sixty, the weatherman had promised. For once, the guy might have it just about right.

With weather that warm, he pulled on jeans, a Hart of Noel T-shirt, and slid an unbuttoned gray flannel shirt over it all. He could remove that later after things warmed up a bit. A head butted his calf as Parnassus, his cat and store mascot urged him to "get a move on." That cat was always trying to get them out the door and into the shop. The crazy animal loved curling up on the mat behind the counter and generally ensuring that Joshua stepped on his tail at least once a day.

"All right. I'm ready. How about you?"

Parnassus did his best attempt at a regal walk to the front door. Considering Joshua had found the animal with one ear chewed off and the other flattened like a Scottish Fold—no relation, the vet had informed him—regality remained only in the cat's wishful thinking.

Some considered him odd for walking the cat from his little house on Sulphur Street, across the railroad tracks and along Gratz to his fallback "dream come true." Hart of Noel—the town's first ever bookstore.

Oh, sure, there'd been antique stores that sold second-hand books. Back in the day, the old Ben Franklin five and dime probably had a spinning rack of paperbacks—most likely bodice rippers and legal thrillers. Maybe Tom Clancy.

The day couldn't have been more beautiful, perfect for having his first "in the black" day since July. Right? Parnassus chased a squirrel but caught up just as they began the trek along the river. Coming up from behind, Joshua opened the back door of the little store that looked more like a house than commercial building, and the cat padded in as if a royal runway. "You sure are full of yourself, Parney."

A flick of the tail told Joshua what Parnassus thought of that. And the day's routine began. The thermostat got bumped from fifty-five to sixty-nine. He raised the blinds, unlocked the cash register, and retrieved his sandwich board and chalks. It had taken him ages to learn how to write on that stupid chalkboard with some semblance of artistry. His niece had been insistent, though. *"People expect it these days. You gotta do what works."*

10

Joshua unlocked the door with his sandwich board wedged under one arm and his baggie of chalk in hand. As the door swung open all good thoughts of the day took a plunge into the Elk River. There it was again, Honey's enormous black SUV parked right in front of his store with her "Honey Potts' Bakery" advertising skins plastered across the windows.

He shot a glare at the bakery across the street where half of Noel had already congregated for their morning infusion of coffee and sugar in the form of pastries, donuts, and the world's best cinnamon rolls, not that he'd ever eaten more than a few dozen himself. In other words, they'd already begun their daily attempt at a diabetic coma.

All right, truth be told, if she weren't his business archnemesis, he'd be over there, too. What could he say? He liked his donuts as much as the next cop—um, guy. But Honey had gone too far.

He'd tried talking to her in person. That's what you did when you had trouble with people. The Bible even said something about it. Her sweet smile had disarmed him, but only until she'd said, "That's what those nice little yellow lines are for, Josh." For the record, he hated being called Josh. "It denotes a *parking* space. I *park* in that *space*."

After that, he'd tried a formal letter requesting that she find some other place to park that didn't block all view of his diminutive store and its equally diminutive sign. Truth be told, her Suburban was nearly as big as his entire store.

Once sent, he wondered if she knew what diminutive meant. Maybe he should have written it in short, simple words that a child could understand.

When his letter had been returned with a cookie, he'd found the words, "To sweeten you up a bit" scrawled on the folded paper. Definitely should have gone for "short and sweet" on those words.

He had gotten his hopes up, though. Because for two whole days she hadn't pulled her black behemoth in front of Hart of Noel. Two whole days!

Granted, one of those days had been Sunday, and instead, she'd parked in his favorite spot at church. To be fair, she didn't know it was his favorite. Nobody did. He had to give her a little leeway on that, but only a little, and only because she had a voice as sweet as her name. Sunday wasn't Sunday if Honey wasn't singing in church.

But now he'd had it. Yep. Things had gone too far. The paperwork had been on his desk for weeks, but Joshua hadn't wanted to do it. Filing that paperwork seemed… drastic. Then again, without something drastic, he may not have a store left to need parking and visibility for. Yes. It was time. He'd send it in, and she'd be forced to park that gas-guzzling titanic somewhere else.

December 1ˢᵗ

Having survived the weekend's ice storm that had left southwest Missouri looking like a fairyland apocalypse, Honey Potts was up and at 'em at four o'clock, getting donuts, fritters, and cinnamon rolls ready for the morning rush. When the doors opened at six, she greeted each customer by name and usual preferred order. "Hey, Luke. Cinnamon roll and a black coffee?"

"And a cranberry white chocolate for Molly."

"Got it!"

A few naysayers had insisted that Noel couldn't support a bakery. Honey had decided to prove them wrong. And she had. She even supplied a few restaurants scattered about McDonald County. *It's all in a positive attitude and a solid marketing plan.*

The Noel Revitalization Project didn't hurt, either. After watching store after store close, the residents and business owners had gotten together to work out strategies to increase the summer tourist trade and try to revive the "Christmas City" spirit. Gayle Hart was even applying for grant after grant for things like park improvements, building upgrades, and who knew what all.

Too bad there isn't a grant for an upgrade on her son's attitude.

Honey glanced at the clock and sighed. She couldn't expect the mail to be in before nine-thirty. Today was the day. The NRP had come up with a genius plan to get customers to visit more stores than ever this Christmas. They'd created a "cooperative lottery," and who she'd been paired with should be waiting for her in her post office box.

Secretly, she hoped for the feed and seed. Dale the owner was such a nice guy. He'd be great to work with, and she could think of all kinds of things they could do together. *Bet Shirley has some good ideas, too.* Shirley always had good ideas. As she said, "Marryin' Dale was just one of the best."

Honey was rooting for more gardens this spring—maybe even people doing a little winter gardening with plastic sheeting and stuff like that. If

13

they could get more produce for the local "Blessings Box," that would be just perfect. A coupon or free packet of seeds and encouragement to help fill the "need it, take it" box over by city hall? What could be better?

An unusual rush came in just before nine-thirty—six people in a row, all chatty, too—so it was almost nine-fifty before Honey grabbed her coat and purse and waved at Emma her morning assistant. It was sign language for, "Off to get the mail. Be right back."

She jogged across the street and climbed into her Suburban. It turned over with a purr that warmed her heart. The seats began warming her backside before she'd pulled out of the parking space and onto Main Street.

Some said that staying in a dying town like Noel was a waste of her talents. Honey said that not resuscitating a town like Noel was a waste of a beautiful opportunity. So she had the sunny optimism of a modern-day Pollyanna. So what? No way was she giving up on her hometown. No how. No way. Nuh uh.

Driving up Main Street, it looked like any other American small town at Christmas. Garland wreaths hanging from light poles, painted windows with winter and Christmas scenes. Ice still clinging to a few trees in the shadier areas.

But for Noel, it was more—much more. In recent years, one by one the traditions had been threatened. One year they hadn't had a tree out on Shadow Lake. Someone had even said they might have to stop the special stamps.

For decades, local volunteers had congregated

14

at the post office, hand stamping card after card with the "Christmas City" wreath or tree. People from all over the country sent cards to the post office to have that stamp on their cards. That tradition wouldn't die if she could help it. Nor would the Christmas tree on Shadow Lake or the parade or... or any of it.

Yes, Christmas in the Ozarks might be a bit of overkill in a town called Noel whose name rhymed with Joel, not Joelle. Well, that was just fine with Honey.

She pulled into the parking space in front of the tiny Noel Post Office and left her engine running as she dashed inside to retrieve her mail. Three catalogs, two utility bills—one for home and one for business—and two letters. The first—from the Noel Revitalization Project. *Yes!*

Honey began tearing it open even as she dashed for her truck. The other letter fell to the floorboard as she closed the door. The return address gave her pause. The City of Noel. *Strange...*

She set the revitalization project letter aside and tore open the one from the city, her gut telling her something was terribly wrong. As she unfolded the letter written on official city letterhead, her stomach sank. "He really did it!"

This is to inform you that the four parking spaces directly in front of the property at 102 Main Street (currently Hart of Noel Books) have been allocated for store customers only. Please ensure your personal vehicle is parked elsewhere. Thank you for your cooperation.

Peg Flannery
City Clerk

Honey balled up the paper and tossed it onto the dashboard just seconds before her brain insisted it couldn't be so. It just couldn't. She reached, stretched, pushed herself, and basically fought to retrieve the wadded-up letter. Maybe the Suburban was overkill after all. Still, she needed the space to deliver her goods.

Letter in hand, she smoothed it out and reread it. Twice. Nope. He really had done it. And some idiot at city hall had let him. What was wrong with those people? No, she didn't blame Peg. Stuff like this had to go before the city council. Why hadn't she been warned so she could be there to present her side?

I'll fight this. All the way to the bank if I have to. Just because my business is thriving while his is floundering is no reason to try to sabotage me. She'd picked that first spot over the bridge for good reason. With the skins on her windows advertising her store—complete with an arrow so folks couldn't miss it—parking anywhere else wouldn't make sense. *What, do I park in front of mine and point the arrow to him? Is that what he wants? I don't* think *so. I paid too much for those skins, and I can't take up parking that actually gets used!*

Oh, yes. She'd fight this.

With her blood pressure soaring to dangerous levels, Honey decided she needed better news to combat the pounding in her ears and extracted the revitalization letter from its envelope. At least Joshua Hart hadn't joined in on this project, or she'd have to worry about being paired with him. She could just hear someone. "Oh, it'd be so perfect. Books and coffee go so well together," Honey quipped in an overly-nasal tone.

With a deep breath and a swift prayer she unfolded it and began to read.

Dear Miss Potts,

The Noel Revitalization Project is excited to announce that you have been paired with—

She stopped reading. This could not be happening. Then again, it was fitting. After all, weren't books and movies full of this same, ridiculous, hackneyed plot? Two enemies forced to work together for the good of the community? Oh, joy.

Scanning the sheet again, Honey picked up where she'd left off. *—Hart of Noel Books for your Christmas in the Christmas City project partner. We will be hosting a potluck at the Methodist Church fellowship hall on December 1 so everyone can help each other brainstorm ideas to ensure the greatest success for this project. Since we got a late start with this idea, we* must *implement it immediately. Looking forward to the best Christmas season Noel has ever had.*

At that point, she quit reading. For good.

Not a big reader herself, Honey didn't know what book said—or was it a movie?— "And the hits just keep on coming," but that phrase now plastered itself in the forefront of her mind. If one more thing went wrong today, she might just throw a honey pot at Joshua Hart the next time she saw him.

Well, she didn't have time to dawdle. She had pies to make for the cafe in Anderson. Risking a scolding or a ticket, she backed the wrong way out of the parking space and headed back toward her bakery. Of course, a train hit just as she reached the tracks. More time to fume and plot her next step. *I wonder if we're allowed to trade. After all, he can't want me any more than I want him. I'll take the funeral home even!*

The train eventually clattered past, and a horn blare behind her jerked Honey out of her reverie. She shot forward and down the rest of Main Street. On auto pilot, Honey started to turn into her usual parking space only to find Joshua Hart pounding signs into the ground in front of his store. Ugly, ugly signs that read—she knew it without even looking at them—Reserved for customers of Hart of Noel only. Violators will be towed.

That funny feeling she got when she was about to do something incredibly brave or utterly stupid rippled through her, and Honey braked right there in the middle of the road. Hands gripping the steering wheel, she stared down Joshua Hart as he gave his sign a final tap with his mallet and stepped back to admire his handiwork. The jerk even waved.

That was too much. She pulled into her usual spot, grabbed her letters and her purse, hopped out, and breezed, "Good morning, Josh! Hungry? I could send someone over with a donut!" And before giving her new enemy a chance to answer, she shoved the letters into her purse and took off across the street.

Two

December 1ˢᵗ

The flat, empty fields of Iowa behind them, Milton Coleridge and his faithful parrotlet, Atticus (not Finch) rolled into Missouri, still uncertain where they'd spend their Christmas. "Austin has some great bookstores, and the weather is supposed to be great. But New Orleans would be something different..."

Truth be told, bookstores didn't sound as appealing as they usually would. He'd planned to spend his Christmas in the charming little town of Red Wing, Minnesota—home of the famous shoes, pottery, and the most adorable Scandinavian shop he'd ever seen. Idyllic.

Even better? Their new and used bookstore, Twice Sold Tales. That place had to make it. The building alone exuded charm. They had customers, events—everything. Why the guy thought the store was in trouble, Milton had never had a chance to find out. The owner had returned after three months of taking care of her dying mother, heard what her stand-in had done, and promptly fired Milton.

"Well, I guess I can't be fired if I wasn't hired, was I? No need to be a pessimist."

Atticus, sitting on the over-the-seat perch, took a step to the right and said, "Sucker." It had taken Milton quite a while to realize the bird really did say it. Every time it came out, it came out the same. Half the time, he tucked it between, "pepper" and "seeds," but considering how often Milton had said, "I'm such a sucker" when handing over another treat, it made sense. Though Atticus didn't have the clear speech of an African Gray, it was becoming apparent that the little guy did talk after all.

They spent the night just outside of Joplin and pulled out by nine o'clock the next morning. According to Google, just out of the way, Southwest City offered a fabulous lunch at The Corner Cafe. "Sounds good to me."

That was one advantage to a life on the road. Sure, it might take you to out-of-the-way little towns, but you also got to see real America—and see just how similar it was in all its diversity.

As they rolled into Southwest City, the first thing Milton noticed was that it shared one thing with most towns in the country—no good parking for a trailer. They'd have to find a side street and hoof it back to the cafe. And with Atticus in his tiny dog carrier, that's exactly what they did.

Lunch? Amazing, but the conversation with a group of ladies at the table next to him almost topped it. "You have to drive over to Noel," one woman said. "I mean, it's the Christmas City, and it's almost Christmas!"

20

He typed in Knoll on his phone and got nothing. "With a W maybe?"

A few titters followed before the woman spelled it out for him. "It's N-o-e-l." She smiled and added, "Well, it's December, so call it No-el if you prefer, but just until Christmas."

Six miles. He could do it. Why not?"

"Darla, you know there's nothing in Noel to interest him. It's just a run-down—" That got the woman a few protests and a glare from Darla that probably gave the woman's children nightmares.

"We're in the middle of a new revitalization project. You go wander around a bit. Check it out."

Revitalization of an entire town instead of one store? Milton couldn't resist. Lots of small businesses waiting for a chance at a brighter future. According to Google, Noel, Missouri had a population of under two thousand.

The chances of a bookstore were slim to none, but still… he'd go see. Learn their stories. Hadn't Paul Ryan once written that "behind every small business there's a story worth knowing"? He'd go learn a few.

Flat fields from nearby Southwest City gave way to rolling hills pretty quickly. Curved roads wound through woods, and he passed a large primary school—well, large for a town of fewer than two thousand people.

As he passed a motel on his left, everything shifted. Large, craggy bluffs formed on his right. A stop sign at a bridge allowed him a moment to enjoy the view. The great bluffs jutted out over the highway—bluffs on the right, the Elk River on the left. "Would you look at that, Atticus? Beautiful."

Atticus chattered about things that probably made sense if you spoke parrotlet. Milton didn't—yet. As far as he knew, Duolingo didn't have that as an option. But now that he knew the bird did try to imitate sounds, he'd pay closer attention. Another bridge took him over the river and into Noel. A black Suburban with window skins pointing to a bakery nearly made him miss the surprise of the day.

"Atticus… books!"

He could have sworn the bird chirped, "Books. Bah."

"Book*store*. Yes." No reason he couldn't choose what the bird said since it was unclear in the first place.

The first parking lot he found, he pulled in and parked his Land Rover and trailer over to one side. Atticus hopped into his carrier the moment Milton pulled out his baggie of bell peppers. Just who had trained whom?

The brisk air hinted that Christmas was on the way. Lights twinkled around the windows of the donut shop across the street. Cars lined up in front of OCH Noel Clinic. But straight ahead, just down from the bank and a food truck promising fusion food… a sandwich board promising free gift wrapping.

It was cold enough that he couldn't stand outside forever, but Milton allowed himself a moment to drink in the charming store. Set back from the road a bit, and with only house letters to spell out the name "Hart of Noel," it was an unassuming little store, and the undersized sandwich board did little to help, especially with that SUV blocking the view.

"Let's check it out, Atticus. I can't believe there's a bookstore here! They really are working to revitalize the town."

The door stuck just a bit as Milton pushed it open. That slight squeak served as an entrance bell. A man rose from behind a counter and smiled at him. "Hi! Welcome to Hart of Noel." At a closer look, he added, "Let me just take Parnassus into the back so he doesn't terrorize your dog."

Odd way of putting it, but Milton didn't argue. When the door shut behind the rather scraggledy-looking creature, he said, "Actually, he might have considered Atticus lunch." He set the carrier down on the counter and gestured at the little screen. "May I?"

"A bird! Haven't seen that before. Sure."

Tallish, broad-shouldered, but otherwise on the scrawnier side, the man sported a short-cropped beard and had the bluest eyes Milton had ever seen—startlingly so, actually. They would have been perfect for a psychopath in a thriller. He laughed—a deep, rich laugh that hinted the man could probably sing, too—at Atticus' flitting from place to place around the little store.

"Cute little thing, but you're right. Parnassus would consider him a nice afternoon snack. Too bad. Wouldn't mind having one like him in the store, but…"

"Great name. From the book?"

"The mountain. Greek mythology. Mount. Parnassus—home of the muses. I thought it might bring me good luck with this store." The guy flushed crimson. "I mean, not that I really believe in luck. I just—it felt—"

23

"I get it. I was thinking of Christopher Morley's book—*Parnassus on Wheels*. Small bookstore…"

"Haven't read that. I'll have to get it. Recent release?" The man sounded hopeful.

It was the first hint that a book crate-sized coffin might need to be ordered.

"Early nineteen hundreds. I assumed a bookseller…" He couldn't resist just one quote. Just one. "'As far as I can see, a man who's fond of books never need starve!'"

"Well, I will if I don't find a way to sell these things."

Uh, oh. Milton glanced over at Atticus and found his bird with head cocked as if listening. Was it his imagination, or did that bird just twitter, "Good books"?

Maybe there was a reason the Twice Sold Tales job had fallen through. Maybe… Still, he'd have to know more, and there was only one way to find out. He thrust out his hand. "Nice to meet you, Mr. Hart?"

The man nodded and took his hand. "Joshua Hart. Owner and starving bookseller."

"Milton Coleridge." How the man responded would likely determine whether Milton stuck around or hightailed it out of Dodge—er, Noel.

"Nice to—really?"

Score one for the bookseller. Milton nodded. "Mom's favorite author, Dad's name, of course. Although, he was a big fan of Coleridge himself."

"As in, 'water, water everywhere' Coleridge? Any relation?"

"Grandma said yes. Dad couldn't trace it, but he was lousy with a computer, so…"

"What brings you to Noel?"

Dare he do it? As Milton considered, Joshua Hart excused himself and went to the window. The expression on the man's face told him something was wrong—terribly wrong. Milton inched a bit to the left and watched as a tow truck blocked the road, hooking up that Suburban.

It's his? Reposessed? Another look of distress on the man's face confirmed it. Especially as it turned hard and grim. *Looks like Austin and New Orleans might just have to wait. We'll see…*

Joshua backed away from the window with a sigh. "Hey, Milton. Warning you. Things are about to get ugly. I'm sorry."

He barely had time to urge Atticus onto his finger before the door flung open. Milton covered the bird with his other hand to prevent an escape as a whirlwind stormed into the store. "You've gone too far, Joshua Hart!"

Uh, oh.

The apology he had begun to formulate withered faster than the evil woman in *Tangled*. Instead, Joshua blurted out, "Well, you got my name right for once. That's an improvement."

"Listen here, *Josh*. I'm not putting up with this. You can't just go around having people's trucks towed."

SUV. The internal correction came instinctively. Joshua ignored it and focused on the situation. "I didn't want to, but a guy has to do

25

whatever he can to save his business. I asked you. I warned you. I went through legal channels. And after further flagrant disregard for the posted sign, I did what I had to do."

"If you wanted to save your business, you would meet with me about our Christmas partnership! But no, you keep putting me off!"

"I didn't sign up for the co-op in the first place." He hadn't meant to admit that. Oops.

Honey blinked at him and then started. "Oh. You have a *customer*. We'll hash this out later. I'm not taking this laying down."

"Lying down."

"What?" Honey threw up her hands and shot a look at Milton. "Sorry about this. Come on over to Honey Potts' Bakery. Coffee and a cinnamon roll are on me."

The door slammed behind her before either man could respond. Joshua turned to face the first non-local customer he'd had since late September. "Hey, she's right. Sorry about that. I should not have let her get under my skin. Again."

Milton released his bird again, just as Parnassus gave a yowl of, "let me in" from the back. "Want me to put Atticus back in his carrier?"

"Parney will survive for a bit. He thinks he's ruler of this domain." Realization dawned. "Atticus! Like in *To Kill a Mockingbird!*"

"I usually say, 'Atticus, not finch.' Not sure why I didn't today. It's not like me. I've even got T-shirts for his fans."

"You have Atticus T-shirts? Is he a trick bird or…?"

"Long story," the man said with that enigmatic

quality that only made the hearer want to know more than ever. "I'll tell you later."

Milton made a slow circuit of his store and stopped at the small display of Spanish titles. "An unexpected selection here."

Everyone thought he was crazy, but he'd sold almost as many Spanish titles to local kids as he had English ones. "We have a good-sized Hispanic community here—lots of parents who don't speak English. Their kids come in and translate for them, but when it comes to buying books, the parents get excited to see Spanish on the shelves."

"You speak Spanish?"

Joshua pulled out his phone and waved it. "I Duolingo it. If anyone ever wants to buy a book about a pink lamp, I'm their man. Still, the kids speak English, so it's a win-win."

"But not a big enough win."

With his counter stool in hand, he gestured for Milton to take the comfy armchair and he plopped himself up on the stool as if an afternoon storyteller. *I guess I'm about to become one.*

"Not yet. I just can't get the tourists in. I thought families coming to the river—the mom needs an escape or maybe the dad's a nerd and isn't into canoeing. Kids need a quiet pastime after a hard day of playing. Stuff like that."

Milton leaned back and held out a finger. Atticus came and perched there as the man stroked the beautiful blue feathers. "You didn't count on America's dependence on screens. Why buy paper and ink when you can have back lighting and five hundred books for half the weight of one?"

"Exactly! I didn't believe them when they said

the independent bookstore is dead." Joshua propped his head on his fist and probably looked a bit too much like *The Thinker* for his own taste. "I hate to think of a world where kids can't walk into a store and be lost in another world before they walk out again. That was my whole childhood."

"Where'd you grow up?"

The guy wouldn't understand. "Here. Born in Anderson. Lived in the same house my whole life until I went off into the Army."

"This store's been here a long time?" Milton didn't sound like he believed it.

"We've never had a bookstore, but Noel has always been a tourist town. Folks come to fish and canoe in the river. They camp over at places like River Ranch. Hike. Explore the Bluff Dweller's Cave. We have a lot to off—" Joshua winced and cut himself off. "Sorry. I can be a walking advertisement sometimes."

Milton scanned the room. "Sink much into this place?"

"My whole military signing bonus. Paid my rent on my house for a year and put the rest in here. I work four nights a week at the chicken plant to pay my personal bills. If I don't find a way to make this place pay…"

After another look around the room, Milton rose. He wandered from section to section as if taking inventory. *Don't tell me to close. I'm going down fighting.*

"You're not much of a fiction reader, are you?"

This was embarrassing. "I like history. Philosophy. Some science stuff. Even a bit of poetry, actually. I've read most of the classics because I figured you'd need to know them. Some were okay.

Not big on genre or popular fiction, but I'm trying. I have a bunch on order at the library."

"How do you choose your titles?"

"Ask around and see what people have been looking forward to." Something in the man's expression told Joshua that Milton didn't agree with that plan. "Why? What would you do?"

"I'd find out what books were like the ones they were looking forward to. Use that app that gives you comparables. 'If you like Dean Koontz, you'll like Ima Arthur.'"

Something told him that made sense, but Joshua couldn't decide why. "Why that rather than the book they want to read in the first place?"

Milton smiled down at Atticus as the bird chirped something. "Yes, good book." He pulled a baggie of what looked like orange bell peppers from his jacket pocket and passed one to the bird. "Joshua, if someone is already looking forward to a book, there's a good chance they've already ordered it or reserved it at the library. You need to find what else they can read while waiting for or have finished reading that book."

It made sense. That didn't help him with a store full of titles he might have to return or sell at a loss, though. "That might just be the shake that wakes me out of my bookstore-owning dream."

"Not necessarily. What you need to do is figure out who liked books that are like the books you bought. Promote those books to those people. And…" Milton hesitated. "Look, do you want to hear this? I can get worked up about business stuff. You don't have to listen."

Something in the man's expression, the way he

spoke, his insights—something said he *should* listen, but why? "Tell me why I should, and I will."

"Because this is what I do. I save companies from bankruptcy and takeovers. And a couple of months ago," he added when Joshua would have broken in and pointed out that tiny bookstores were a far cry from companies. No one was waiting to take over his store unless it was Honey. To close it. "A couple of months ago, I helped a bookstore in a town half this size save itself from closing. They're doing really well right now. I have testimonials."

And there was the rub. "Sorry, guy. I can't afford you. Even if you worked for a dollar an hour, I couldn't afford you. I've got to get through Christmas and see if the holiday helps at all because January—"

"Is a time for new resolutions. People need self-help books for all those. They vow to read more. You provide the books. You have to stop thinking about the customers coming to you and start figuring out how you can go to the customer. Solve a pain point, and they'll be in here. I'm sure of it. This town is determined to thrive."

Joshua listened, ideas whirling in his mind. "Still can't afford you, but I'll take that advice and try to use it. Thanks."

"I never said I'd charge you a dime."

A dime… something about that hinted…and then Joshua got it. "What *will* you charge me?"

"Your trust." Milton gave him a wry smile. "It's more expensive than money, and it won't be easy to pay. You're not going to like some of what I say, but will you be willing to trust that I wouldn't waste hours, that I get paid *very* well for by the way, telling

30

you to do things that won't work."

The worst thing about fiction was always the subtext. Joshua usually could interject several different possibilities into it, and some of those would often contradict each other. This conversation had just shifted into subtext, and he had no idea what he'd missed. Then again, what did he have to lose? His mom did his books and every week she showed his bank account dwindling at rates that made the 1929 stock market crash look like a blip.

His voice cracked in a way it hadn't since he was fifteen as he said, "If I can do it, I will. I'll try anything within reason, and you seem…" He tried to laugh, but it came out as an even more embarrassing squeak. "Reasonable. Where do we start?"

Milton rose and carried Atticus to his carrier. With the bird tucked away inside, he pointed to the door. "You let Parnassus have his domain back for a while, and I'll go have my free coffee and cinnamon roll." Milton gazed at him for a moment. "Will I like it?"

"Best ever." And Joshua had managed not to sound begrudging when he said it, either.

"I'll be back. I have some thinking and reconnaissance to do."

31

Three

Bees. Of course, the decor of Honey Potts' Bakery focused on bees. It had begun, or so Milton suspected, with the black and white commercial tile. It wasn't new, so she'd obviously decided to work with what she had. White walls—a relief from the expected yellow—sported little decor. Aside from a quote scattered along the top of one wall that read, *"But I would feed you with the finest of the wheat, And with honey from the rock I would satisfy you. ~Psalm 81:16"*, the only wall decor came in the form of black framed artwork with a hand-drawn bee and below it, hand-lettered reminders such as "bee kind" and "bee grateful." Milton counted seven in all. A tiny note tucked into the frame on each read, "unframed prints available."

"They're adorable, aren't they?"

The voice behind him had to be Honey's. Without turning to greet her, he nodded. "So simple but powerful."

"I saw this Rae Dunn cannister that said, 'Bee Sweet.' I wanted the simplicity of it, but something more original, so I hired one of the high school girls to make them. I sell prints for her, because the twenty bucks each that I spent wasn't really worth her time. She spent days perfecting that tiny bit of wash under the lettering and redoing each one over and over until it was good enough."

"Does she sell many?"

Honey adjusted the "bee loving" frame a fraction of a centimeter as she explained the difference between summer and winter crowds. "I sold at least ten a week in July and August. Now we're lucky to get one or two. But Christmas is coming. I'm going to tack up little cards that say things like, 'a perfect gift for a teacher' near them."

One advantage Milton had as a short man was the way he rarely looked down at a woman. Something about that gave him a different perspective, or so he liked to think. Honey Potts would be an interesting person. Something in those amber eyes the exact color of dark honey—could her parents have been prescient?—told him there was far more to this animosity with Joshua Hart than met the eye. But what?

He thrust out his hand. "Milton Coleridge. Nice to meet you Miss Po—"

"Honey. Everyone calls me Honey."

Milton waited for the comment about his name, but it never came. Interesting. Instead, he asked the name question. "Your full name or a nickname?"

"Nickname."

He'd thought so. No one with the surname of Potts would be so cruel. "I see."

"No, you don't." Those amber eyes grew even warmer, if possible. "My real name is Honeydew."

You are too young for hippie parents. Wannabes?

34

Honey burst out laughing and beckoned him to the front. "Let's get you some coffee. Plain, black, a bit of sugar?"

"Yes." But Milton stopped her before she could reach for a mug. "Unless you have a house drink you want me to try. I like being adventuresome, too."

"Gotcha. A Honey Pot Latte coming up. And my name… My mother named us after cravings. You have no idea how grateful I am that she didn't want watermelon or cantaloupe."

She wanted him to ask. That was obvious. Milton obliged. "And that 'we' includes…"

Laughter rang out loud, brash, like a female James Corden. Beautiful. "You catch on fast. My oldest brother… Tony." At his raised eyebrow, she shrugged. "Okay, so it's Festoni, but only because Dad put his foot down and refused to let Mom name him Ziti. Can you imagine? A teen boy?"

Is she teasing—no. No, she's not.

"Even better, her second choice was gnocchi. Dad said he'd find a pasta that worked. He chose either Festoni or Vesuvio. And the rest is history."

"Just the two of you?"

She worked on autopilot. While she mixed and frothed, Honey talked, and without the strong accent that Joshua had. *So not from around here?*

"Four. I'm the baby, of course. Festoni, Colby, Sherbert, and Honeydew."

She said sherbet with the R so many people added—indicative   of   another   boy,   or mispronunciation? Milton didn't know how to ask. "What does…" He forced himself to say it in case it had been spelled that way on the birth certificate, "Sherbert go by?"

35

"Sher—like the actress. She threatens to legally change her name to it all the time. Colby and I are the only ones who don't pitch a fit about our names." Honey set a plate with a cinnamon roll that could have been ripped from a magazine in front of him. "Sher says, 'That's because yours sounds like an endearment, and Colby's is at least normal.'" She leaned forward, arms resting on the low counter. "No one ever told her that Colby's name would have been Havarti if he'd been a girl. Dad put his foot down on Muenster, too."

She retrieved a steaming coffee cup, slapped a lid on it, and slid a custom sleeve up from the bottom. That sleeve said, "Bee Sweet." Honey tapped it. "I had her do these, too. Because, come on! Oh," she added as he inspected it. "And because I can tell you're too polite to ask but you really want to know, Dad didn't put his foot down about the names in general because he says when a woman has to go through the agony of pushing out a honeydew, she has the right to name it almost anything."

A few customers came in, so Milton found himself a place in the corner and took his first bite of cinnamon roll. Wow. He'd have to bring one back for Joshua. The guy would need the fortification.

Between sips of a latte that hinted of cinnamon, honey, and… apple? Milton took another sip. Definitely apple. He continued his appraisal of the room. She'd probably gotten the nineties golden oak tables and carved back chairs dirt cheap at garage and estate sales. It looked like the furniture showroom his mother had drooled over before deciding to save for her own set.

And thank You, Lord, that she couldn't save enough

until they were out of style.

A young woman came out, wiping wet hands on a towel, and Honey pointed his way. A nod, a smile, and the girl stepped up to the register to take the next order. Honey practically ran to his table. "What do you think?"

"Amazing. I'll have to have this every day I'm here—and then a ten-mile walk to work it off."

She beamed. A phone call interrupted them, and from the sound of it, she was in negotiations to have her fine waived. "I'll pay Joe. It's not his fault. He did the work. But I really don't think I should have to pay a fine for something that is new, and I just received notice of today." A smile spread across her face. "Thanks, Peg."

As she disconnected, Honey tapped the back of the chair opposite him. "Mind if I sit?"

"Please do, and maybe you can tell me about this partnership with Joshua."

He hadn't expected it to be so easy, but Honey laid it all out. "I have good ideas, too. I don't know what will work for his deal, but I was thinking that we want to evoke good memories and traditions. So, for every book he sells, he can give them a coupon for a free Christmas ornament cookie. I mean, nothing says Christmas like ornaments and cookies, right? I'll just combine them."

"Sounds good to me. It's not too expensive?"

Honey wilted faster than a violet in the desert. "The way his store is going, I won't have to give away more than one or two. I wish I could help."

He'd make an enemy of her, but Milton had a responsibility toward Joshua now. "You can."

She sat upright, hands flat on the table. "What?

37

What can I do? Maybe he'll get off my back if I actually *help*."

"You won't like it."

Never had he seen someone show such extremes before. The wilted Honey sagged into the chair, her arms drooping at her sides. "My truck."

"It blocks the view of his store. If I hadn't been crawling past, trying to take in everything, I would never have seen it. Your Suburban blocks it. Even if you just parked five spaces over, it would help, but then you'd block the food truck."

That droop tilted forward, forehead resting on the tabletop now. "I need that arrow pointing this way. And I paid a fortune for those skins before Hart of Noel was ever a twinkle in Josh's eye."

She didn't seem naturally selfish, so Milton just waited for her to figure it out on her own. It took less time than it took for him to chew his next bite of cinnamon roll. "I have to do it, don't I?"

"Have? Yes. It's enforceable. But what about 'should'?"

As if once the decision had been made, everything had been resolved, Honey jumped up. "Just a minute. Be right back."

She returned a minute later with a small pastry box in hand, the Honey Potts' Bakery logo slapped on top with a sticker. "Take this over to Josh, will you? Tell him I'll keep my truck over in the Harps parking lot. Out of the way."

Milton used his fork to point to the box. "I'll need to buy one to go as well. I may not be able to wait until morning for another one. Oh," he added before she could jump up again. "I think I know how to compromise on the signage."

"Anything! Please!"

"Let me talk to Joshua first."

That stopped her. "Wait… did he hire you to help with his marketing or something?"

"I volunteered. It's what I do, and I like bookstores. So…" He shrugged. "I needed a Christmas project."

The "business mode" Honey returned. She sat up a bit straighter and put on a professional smile. "Well, if you can get Josh to work with me, that would be a miracle. I should have known Mrs. Hart had something to do with him signing up, but I just thought desperation struck." She gave him an apologetic smile before adding. "People don't read anymore. The bookstore is dead. Read the papers and the internet. They all say the same thing. Paper books are out."

"And yet I just saved a store in a town of a couple hundred people from closing. They're thriving." He grinned over his coffee cup at the shock on her face. "*You* may not read, Miss Potts, but many, many people do. I think there's hope for this store, yet."

"Save it, then. I want him to succeed, even if only to prove I'm not his enemy." Honey leaned forward and whispered, "Do you know he was having a good time at the planning potluck until he saw me? He took one look, stared, and turned away. Avoided me all night. And over a parking space?"

Over a business, most likely, but you can't see that yet. That's okay. Baby steps, as they said. He'd just have to take those baby steps. "When are you available to talk about this Christmas partnership thing?"

"If you can get him over here after closing

tonight, I'll go over to the BBQ place and get us pulled pork sandwiches." She hesitated. "Want one? Ribs? Burger?"

He pulled out his wallet and slid a twenty across the table. "Pulled pork, please, but I'll take mine to go. You guys need to work out your troubles without me getting in the way."

She started to protest and push the money back, but he leaned back, arms folded over his chest, and shook his head. "No… really. I owe you for the extra cinnamon roll, and I want to feel free to ask you to do it again if you're going somewhere. I won't if I'm afraid you'll be too generous. That just makes me a burden."

After considering him for a moment, Honey rose and picked up the bill. "I'll keep it and your change in an envelope. Whenever you want something, you just let me know. I'll get that cinnamon roll." When she returned, Honey added, "And if you're interested, we do potlucks at church on Wednesdays. You're welcome to come. No contribution needed. We always have plenty."

"Where and what time?"

"Church of Christ on Kings Highway and Short Street. Six-thirty."

He'd probably be there, but he wouldn't tell her that. Not yet.

four

That little bird chattered nonstop until Joshua went and got the carrier and put him on the counter. From his window, he could see Milton and Honey in deep conversation. Would the man return and rescind his offer of help? Joshua almost feared so. He also feared the fate of little Atticus if Parnassus got a hold of him. The cat sat with one eye on the carrier and one paw ready to swipe.

Through the window of his store, Joshua watched the conversation between Honey and Milton, confused at the half-dozen emotions showing in half as many minutes. She looked her usual bubbly self one minute, drooped the next, dropped to the table, and back up again. "Atticus, either your guy is a miracle worker, or Honey has finally gone off the deep end."

Parnassus batted his arm and hopped down off the counter in a snit.

By the time Milton arrived, cinnamon roll in hand, he'd convinced himself that Honey would have

41

the man won over to her side in the parking space war. The door hadn't even shut behind him before Joshua pounced. "Well?"

Milton passed the cinnamon roll across the counter. "For you. From Honey. She says she'll be parking at Harps from now on. She gets it now."

The guy was a miracle worker. "I'm tempted to buy you a lottery ticket. You'd probably win."

"Don't waste your money."

His fingers tingled and his heart kicked up a notch. This might work. "So... what next?"

Milton greeted Atticus first before leaning against the counter and tapping the box. "You should eat that. You're going to need fortification." The moment Joshua took a bite, Milton asked, "Want to tell me what happened at the potluck?"

Uh oh. *What'd she say?*

"You should know, Honey thinks you were so upset about the parking space that just seeing her ruined your night."

"Not hardly."

His face flamed at Milton's nod and when the guy said, "That's what I thought."

The "Open" side of the sign winked at him. Joshua jumped up to fix it and buy himself a bit of time. How could he explain to Milton what he didn't understand himself?

"I want to say, 'It's your decision whether you want to talk about it,' but I don't think we have time for you to work through your issues at leisure."

So much for the "I'm not comfortable talking about it right now" approach. Instead, in a bid for just another minute of life pre-mortification, Joshua turned the conversation back on Milton. "What'd she tell you?"

"Something to the effect that you looked like you were having fun until you saw her. She believes you avoided her all night because of the parking space."

"I wish."

"Again," Milton said. "I suspected."

Rip off that Band-Aid. One quick rip. "She wore a new dress—green. She looked great, and I noticed it." A glance over at Milton showed the guy just watching him. He sighed. "Yeah, maybe it was a bit juvenile, but I didn't know how to handle attraction to someone I'd cheerfully throttle if it weren't against the law—and permanent. So, I just avoided her to keep from doing or saying something *really* stupid."

Milton stood and stretched. He set Atticus' carrier on the counter and scanned the room as if trying to decide where to begin. "Do you have any paper?"

That's it? No matchmaker, "You should ask her out. Maybe she's the one," or philosopher, "It's just a biological response built into humans through evolutionary somethings" mumbo jumbo? Either way, he'd take it. Josh pulled a legal pad from a drawer and passed it and a Bic pen over.

Milton pulled a small pen from his pocket and unscrewed the cap. A fountain pen. Of course, someone like Milton would eschew such plebeian pens. "Carry my favorite with me, but thanks." As he drew a line down the middle of the page, Milton said, "Well, you'll be pleased to know Honey is wearing leggings and a Honey Potts T-shirt."

And why do I care what she's wearing today? Since Milton obviously hadn't yet learned to read minds,

43

Joshua asked just as Parnassus hopped up on the counter and eyed Milton's pen.

"Because you're eating dinner with her after you close. Pulled pork sandwiches, so if you don't like those, you'd better call and tell her what you want." At the bottom third, Milton drew a line across the page. "All right. What's more pressing—this shop or this co-op thing?"

"If I'm going to Honey's, then the co-op. I never wanted to do that, but my mom's a big part of the revitalization committee, so I get roped into everything."

Milton nodded. "Families have a way of doing that... and then one day, they aren't there to do it anymore."

Remember to hug Mom before you go home. Since Milton didn't say anything else, Joshua let it drop. "So, what do you think we should do? I mean, she can't give away her cinnamon rolls to everyone who buys a book, or I'd be rich, and she'd be broke—not how I wanted to get that Suburban moved."

"She's recommending sugar cookies made to look like ornaments. She says they aren't expensive, but she thinks people would like them. I agree with her."

"And what do I give? I can't get away with giving away books unless I go buy a ton at an estate sale, wrap them, and people get a grab bag book—which I can't afford, but I could pull fifty bucks from my emergency fund if I *had* to."

"I think we'll use those dollars for something else."

That's what I was afraid of.
"Here's my thought."

44

With that, Milton began talking and writing at dizzying speeds. He laid out a plan that Joshua had to admit might just work. It offered more than the co-op freebie or discount idea. It actually added in incentive to shop.

When Joshua agreed, the little man grabbed his phone and began flipping through it. A moment later, he shoved it across the counter and said, "Will that suit you?"

"Sure, but…"

"Do you know anyone who does this kind of cutting here who can match or beat that price—*fast*?"

He thought for a minute and pulled out his phone, keeping the page open on Milton's. "Hey, Derek? Don't you have one of those wood laser cutters?" When Derek said he did, Joshua just handed over the phone and went to suck his thumb in the corner.

Actually, he picked up Parnassus and gave the cat long back scratches, but for them, it was basically the same thing.

The door jangled shut behind Milton, leaving Josh and Honey all alone. "Um…" A bout of nerves hit her before Honey could blurt out the apology she'd been rehearsing all afternoon. It galled to have to do it, but she'd taken a walk down to the highway, turned around, and walked back. Even without her truck parked there, she could see he'd been right. It would have blocked that store sign and half the store.

"Do you have somewhere you want us to work

45

or…?" Joshua's mellow voice didn't boom out in the room like so many men's did, but it did fill the air with a sort of warmth.

"Well, we can sit at the long table, of course, or we can go sit in back if you don't want the town spying on us or trying to get in for the last donut."

"Cinnamon roll." He grinned. "They'd be coming for your cinnamon rolls. And thanks for sending that. Hit the spot, especially since I'd forgotten to bring my lunch."

She picked up the bag of food from Smokin' BBQ and led him through the back to her office. It wasn't a big room, but she had created a desk out of a six-foot folding banquet table and crafty cubbies set about it so she could put her monitor on top of one, her printer on another, and still have room to work on bill paying, invoices, and all that admin stuff. The other end often served as a breakroom table, assembly counter, or dump spot during busy times.

"Have a seat. I'll get us some napkins. Want a Coke or a Mountain Dew? That's all anyone drinks around here. Except sometimes Emma makes sweet tea. I could bring that."

"Coke's fine. Thanks."

When she returned, a ten-dollar bill lay across the workspace of her desk. Milton's words about feeling free to ask without worry stopped her from pushing it back to Joshua. She did, however, hold it up. "I meant for this to be my treat—a peace offering." Honey swallowed hard. "I took a walk today. Came up on your side of the street." She popped open her Coke and took a swig before adding, "I'm sorry, Josh. I didn't get it. I thought—"

"That's all right. We'll work this out." Josh

poked at his sandwich. "Do we want to pray or…?"

"Sure! Thanks."

You'd think after three years, Honey would be used to this praying thing, but while at home and at church felt so natural she'd have squirmed if someone *didn't* pray before a meal, she still hadn't gotten used to prayers in "public" places, and in her mind, her store fit that description.

Her apology did not loosen Josh's tongue. They ate in near total silence until at least half his sandwich was gone. Hers took longer. Either he was hungrier, or she'd become a slowpoke eater. *Guess it's up to me.*

"So, did Milton tell you my cookie idea?"

After a chew, a swallow, and a swig of Coke, Josh wiped his mouth with his napkin and nodded. "Sure did, although he thinks you should make a change to your cookie shape."

"But the ornament thing is the whole idea—the tie-in to Christmas. I'm not doing anything crazy fancy. I have a couple of tear-drop styled bulb cutters and gingerbread—"

"Honey?"

He'd said her name before. She knew he had to have said it. But his mellow tones, that slow, sing-song accent the locals had… her name almost sounded like it had three syllables and dripped with the stuff. Honey, that is. The awkward, uncomfortable thought that she could listen to him say her name all day scattered any comfortable vibes they'd managed to create, though there weren't many.

"Hmm?"

"Can I tell you his idea before you shoot it down? Might as well know what you're aiming for."

If he hadn't been smiling at her, Honey might

47

have squashed the rest of her pulled-pork sandwich on his head—or at least dumped her slaw there. "Sorry. Let me have it—gives me more time to formulate a great argument anyway."

"That's the spirit." This time the guy winked. Even weirder, he turned red under that beard of his almost the moment he did it.

You don't know how to people, do you? That's been your trouble all along. How's Milton going to fix that?

"He thinks the ornament idea is a great one—just had me order more wood cut out ornaments than I can afford as my giveaway. They're books."

Honey blinked. Book ornaments? Who'd want those?

She'd either spoken aloud or her question burned in her eyes, because Josh shook his head and said, "Milton said you'd wonder who'd want a book ornament." He pulled out his phone and used his thumb to unlock it. There on the open screen was a shopping page of book-themed ornaments. "Readers, Honey. There's a lot of us in this world."

Keep calling me Honey in that tone and I'll become one myself. When that thought fully registered, Honey shot a look at him to make sure she wasn't speaking aloud. He'd returned to his slaw. When had he eaten half the stuff? "Got it. Readers. So, you'll have ornaments and I'll have…?"

"Bee cookies. Milton says you want your giveaway to be something that links people to your store in their memories. They remember that good cookie, it was a bee, so they want to go to the bee bakery and get one of Honey Potts' cookies, although I'd recommend those cinnamon rolls."

Oh, she hated how right he was. At least it was

Milton instead of Josh. She could thank the Lord for huge, pride-saving favors. "I have a cookie cutter…" She dug around in two cubbies, three drawers, and a basket under the table before she found it. "I can order a couple more so we can cut faster. I'll put two to a goodie bag. Perfect. What do my folks need to buy to get the ornament from you?"

Josh just grinned.

"Dumb question. Okay, buy a coffee and a cinnamon roll or two or more cinnamon rolls and get an ornament?"

"No. Buy a box of cinnamon rolls. Milton swears people will do it. They like to get free stuff and have justification for buying more of what they already want."

A box of cinnamon rolls… that was nine rolls. Twelve bucks. Honey eyed him. "What do people have to buy to get two bee sugar cookies?"

"A book for…" He scrunched up his face as he tried to pronounce something she couldn't comprehend, even if it would save a cinnamon roll from landing on the floor. "Yole-ah-bouke-a-flod." After saying it twice more, Josh pulled out his phone and found another website. "There."

Honey stared at the screen. *Jolabokaflod*. Beside it the translation: Christmas book flood.

"I guess there wasn't paper rationing during World War II in Iceland, so they did this big marketing thing where they sent a book catalog to everyone in the country. It became a thing to buy books for people on Christmas. They open their presents on Christmas Eve in Iceland, so lots of people stay up late reading their new books."

"And you're going to try to get the people of

this town to... buy books? Have a contest on who can butcher that word worst? What?"

"Books. Milton has a list of twenty-five blog posts I have to have written by Friday."

That threw her. "I didn't know you had a blog."

"I don't... yet." He glanced at his phone. "Or maybe I do by now. Milton said he'd set up the website and blog during his dinner. It'll be super basic, but with a couple of plug-ins and widgets, it should be ready to launch by morning."

A low buzzing filled her ears. Honey shook her head and pushed her sandwich away. "Did any of that make sense to you?"

Josh downed the rest of his Coke in one gulp, swallowed a burp (bless him), and wiped his mouth with his napkin. Seriously, Honey expected him to announce, "All done!" Instead, he said, "Nope. Not a clue, but Milton obviously does."

"He's gotta be expensive, Josh. Can you afford this?"

"I looked him up." Josh pulled out that phone again. How'd she never notice how much he used that thing? A moment later, he passed it over.

Honey read. If her eyes bulged as much as it felt like they did, he'd be calling for the paramedics. "Whoa... He's worked with some huge companies. The way they're talking, he must make more in a month than I do in a year."

"Stands to reason," Josh argued. "He can't be guaranteed any business in a year, much less something every month."

That was true. She read the next screen he showed her—a Facebook group for independent bookstores. Some gal in California credited him for

50

saving their store from closing.

"I think if he can keep me afloat through April, I'll make it with the improvements and changes he's mentioned so far. It's all about showing people who want something that you have it. I've been trying to figure out how to convince people who don't want to read that they need to buy books. Wrong approach."

"I'll say. Some of us just don't enjoy reading."

That slow smile and his piercing eyes—man those eyes and those eyelashes were so not fair—unsettled something in her. Honey knew what the moment he said, "I'm making it my personal goal to change that—for you, I mean."

"Good luck. You're going to need it."

She'd have driven him home, but Josh said Parnassus, the evil-looking cat, looked forward to their daily walks. "He likes to terrorize the neighborhood dogs."

"He looks like a dog terrorized *him*."

"He lived to fight another day," Josh said in a flat, serious tone that Honey didn't know what to do with.

They stood at the edge of Main Street, and the former awkwardness descended like a family secret blurted out by a five-year-old. Josh took the first step away. Then he froze, standing in the street. "Where's your SUV?"

"Harps lot." He jerked his head. "Come on, then. I'll walk you down. It's not safe walking after dark here anymore."

As sweet as it was, it wasn't necessary. A block away on the main drag through town? Even she didn't feel jumpy about it. "That's not necessary. I'll be doing it every day anyway."

51

He still fell into step beside her. "Then I'll walk with you every day that you leave after dark."

In an attempt to wake him up to reality, she tried again. "I arrive before light, Josh. It's really not necessary."

That earned her a look. "What time do you come down?"

"By four, usually."

At her truck, he hesitated. "Do you have my number?"

"It's in the church directory, isn't it?" Of all the weird things. Josh Hart took the time to put his phone number into her contacts. "Text me when you leave for work. I'll meet you here."

"No! That's—"

"Either text me, or I'll start waiting for you at three. Night."

Honey stood there watching until he went around the bank and disappeared. "He's lost his mind."

five

December 3rd

After setting down the two-liter bottles of soda, his standard offering for the weekly church potluck, Joshua surveyed the dishes and detected a Mexican theme. The ladies were great about coming up with a general meal plan for each week, but he never paid attention until he dropped off the drinks. It was nice to be surprised.

Honey barreled into the room with a bowl in her hands, chattering a mile a minute to poor Mrs. Arnott, and Joshua's throat went dry. It wasn't the same dress—this was more like a long shirt. They had a word for it. His mother wore them all the time, though not nearly as well, he decided. But aside from length and color—this was a deep purple—Honey might as well have been wearing the dress from the potluck.

And it shook him just as hard. He couldn't deny it any longer. Honey Potts was an attractive woman. Too bad she was an annoying one, too.

He had to get out of there. Now. It had snowed

53

all afternoon—a good two inches for sure. *Better shovel it before it becomes a chore.*

Weaving through the clusters of chatterers gathering in the little fellowship hall, Joshua grabbed his coat from the back of his chair and slipped outside before anyone could ask him what he was up to. It didn't take but a minute to unlock the shed, grab the shovel, and begin clearing a path all around the building. Sure, no one came in the front door on Wednesday nights, but leaving snow there was just asking for a thaw and freeze that would result in ice.

The things a guy will tell himself to justify… whatever needs justification. Besides, his mother hadn't gone in for cold showers and coddling. She believed in hard work to burn off all the unsettling emotions. If it worked as a teen, why not a thirty-something?

A tap on his shoulder, and Honey's, "Hey, Josh" nearly sent the shovel flying with the scoop of snow.

"What are you doing? I could have thrown that into Mrs. S's truck!"

"I need to talk to you."

He chanced a look at her and saw her wrapped in that coat that looked like it belonged to the gal in Carmen San Diego. *Whew.* Despite his relief, Joshua kept shoveling. It wouldn't hurt. "What's up?"

"The sign. Milton said he had an idea for a sign that would help both of us. It's been two days! I really need—"

"We're at church, Honey." When she didn't respond, Joshua relaxed. Finally. Respite.

He relaxed a bit too soon. "Yeah. I can see that. Thanks for telling me. So, about the sign, what—?"

Joshua slammed the shovel down on the

concrete, let the force jolt through him to steady himself, and faced her. "Look. I need a Switzerland." Her blank expression told him he needed to elaborate. "I need a safe place—somewhere that business and all its irritations don't intrude. That needs to be here. I need to know I can walk into that door and not have to worry if I can pay the light bill or if turning the thermostat down two degrees will keep people out."

"Great. You're not inside, so—"

"I need it now. Right now. Right here."

"And I need a sign!"

As if granted one by the Lord Himself, Milton walked around the corner and waved. "Hey! I tried to get in, but the door's locked."

Honey would have dashed over to Milton right then, but Joshua caught the sleeve of her coat. "I meant it, Honey. Don't bug me about business at church." His mother's training kicked in, and he tacked on, "Please."

The tension sizzled with the crackle of a summer thunderstorm. Milton decided he should remind his new "clients" that they were on the same team now. "Hey, my two favorite people in town." He winked at Honey's snort and added, "Okay, so the only two people I know, but it's still true. While I have you both here, can we meet in the morning before the bakery opens to talk signage?"

"Don't mention anything to do with business while you're on sacred ground." Honey's words were not sweet, soft, or sticky. They held a razor edge that he'd rather never be on the receiving end of. "Someone considers this place above the carnality of filthy lucre." She shot Joshua a look. "Just because I don't read much doesn't mean I'm an idiot."

The door slammed shut behind her before Milton realized she'd stalked off. A look at Joshua showed a defeated man. Joshua leaned on the shovel, eyes closed, and steadied himself. "She knows how to get under my skin."

"Want to talk about it?"

"Not really." Joshua shot him a weak but growing grin. "You asked."

"So I did." Milton stared at the door as Byron's poem came to mind. "'She walks in beauty…' in the night?"

The man gave the shovel another shove, prompting Milton to wonder if the word "shove" fit into the etymology. He'd never thought of it that way. More to the point, he noted that when a man is shoveling a couple of inches of snow in the dark, it only stands to reason something upset him before he came outside.

"You're a bit unnerving, Milt. Just so you know."

Though he truly despised "Milt" as a nickname—nicknames in general, actually—this time Milton chose to correct someone to diffuse tension. *That's a first.* He cleared his throat. "Um, you know how you hate Josh?"

"Milton. Got it."

A man stuck his head out the door and called to them. "We're about ready to eat. You don't need to shovel that little bit, Joshua. We're fine."

56

Both men returned the shovel to the shed. As they walked back to the building, Joshua sighed. "She's got a shirt that's just like that dress. I had to get out of there, and then she followed me out there, yammering about some sign. I just asked for one place where I didn't have to think about how to make a buck." He reached for the doorknob. "Is that really too much?"

"No." Milton held the door as it swung open. "But I think we both know that she probably picked up on there being more to it than that."

A few people milled about by the door, but that didn't stop Joshua from murmuring, "Did she have to be so annoying? The combo is just cruel."

Margaret Wolfe Hungerford might have crafted the phrase, "Beauty is in the eye of the beholder," but Honey Potts of Noel, Missouri personified it. What Joshua saw in her, he couldn't tell. It wasn't that the woman was *unattractive*. She wasn't. But in Milton's opinion, she was hopelessly ordinary. Average height, average weight, average features…

Honey came into view. The purple tunic she wore? Beautiful. And it flattered her. However, Milton didn't see anything in it so remarkable as to unsettle any man. Any man except Joshua Hart, bookseller.

There'd been another couple at the last bookstore he'd helped. Although Milton liked to joke with them that he'd played the successful matchmaker, the truth was both parties had been interested long before his arrival. This time he had only a few weeks and two people with obvious chemistry—of all the wrong sort.

But magnets can both attract and repel. What if I can

57

figure out how to flip them around so they stop pushing each other away…?

Those thoughts—they'd have to wait. In seconds, the little congregation at the Noel church of Christ welcomed him in as if he were family who had come home after a long time away. Someone asked why he was there, and Milton could have sworn Honey muttered something about not asking while Josh was around.

Those ladies, like church ladies the world over, knew how to cook. Enchiladas, some casserole, build your own tacos, a taco salad, salsa and chips… He'd have to figure out what he could bring next week.

A pang shot through his heart. One enormous drawback to his life—no home church. He kept in touch with his parents' old church back in Oregon. Everyone needs spiritual accountability. But few people realized the gift that is a home church where you knew you'd be week after week.

"Who has a song they'd like to start with?"

Joshua leaned close and murmured, "You're in for a treat. Wait'll you hear her sing."

Milton didn't have to ask who "her" was.

A little girl whispered to her mother, and her mother spoke up. "Hannah wants to sing sixty-eight."

Milton flipped open *Sacred Selections* to the proper page and smiled. "Count Your Blessings."

In all his travels, one thing Milton had learned was that you could count on great harmony anytime you entered a church of Christ. Well, almost anytime. There'd been that tiny church in southwestern Oklahoma. Ten people at most, half of them tone deaf and the other half terrified to sing with all that

58

racket. Still, they'd made a truly joyful noise—those who did sing.

One by one, this group sang songs he hadn't heard in months—some of them in years. And Joshua hadn't exaggerated. Honey Potts could make a mean cinnamon roll, and the woman could sing. A man could fall in love with a voice like hers. The minister, Luke, kept saying, "Oh, the singing's good tonight. Let's just do one more."

Milton couldn't resist. "Do you ever do…" He checked where his finger held his place. "One hundred three?"

"Oh, 'A Beautiful Life.'" Luke nodded to the guy leading the singing.

That's when Milton noticed the grin on most of the faces. Joshua shot him a look and whispered, "Best choice possible."

And it was true. While the singing had been wonderful, something about that song brought out the best in everyone. Even Honey managed to step it up a notch, and after the end of the final chorus, the song leader started the chorus over one more time as if unwilling to let it end.

Luke pulled his Bible toward him and said, "Well, last week we were looking at I Corinthians thirteen. We've looked at patient and kind… but what about verse five? I thought we'd go over that one a bit tonight. Joshua, could you read that verse out to us?"

The man took a swig of his soda, choked, and began in a strained voice, "'…does not act unbecomingly; it does not seek its own, is not provoked, does not take into account a wrong suffered.'"

December 4th

S o she'd gone a little bit overboard and made a quiche Lorraine. Anything to keep Josh Hart from going off on her again. Who did he think he was? Mr. "I'm too spiritual to talk business at church." It was just a simple question. *All he had to do was say, "I don't know." What is so hard about that?*

Still, the lesson had hit home and hard— particularly that little bit about love not being "self-seeking." OOPS. Yeah… Honey had spent half the night justifying herself as being a "good steward of her business" and "looking out for the needs of her customers."

She almost believed it, too.

True to his word, despite his obvious irritation with her, Josh had been waiting at the parking lot at three o'clock when she arrived to get a head start. How'd he known? Guilt prodded her into saying, "Hey… next time I'll just park by my store and move my truck later. There's no need for you to get up like this." Honey winced. *How gracious of you.* "But thanks.

61

Really. It's awful sweet of you."

His grunt annoyed her until he yawned and added, "Sorry. What? Still trying to keep the eyelids open. I stayed up way too late workin' on those ornaments."

After repeating her moment of gratitude, Honey said, "What're you doing to the ornaments?"

"They come cut out, but they're plain, you know? Just wood. So I'm going to write 'Hart of Noel Books' in tiny block print on the back. So far, all I've done is stain the fronts to show creases for the middle and the pages. Then I'll write 'Books are gifts of the heart' on the little pages of the ornament."

It sounded complicated to her. "Did you get enough to sell? People might like to buy one to tie onto a ribbon. Oh, and maybe instead of painting 'Hart of Noel Books' on the back, print out a label with your store address and website. Do it on a removable sticker so folks can peel it off and put it in their planner or journal or something."

Josh didn't respond until they reached the bakery, but he smiled at her when she got the door open and turned on the light. "Great idea. Thanks. That'll save ages. Or at least until the rubber stamp I bought with my website name on it comes. Then I can just stamp that. They can get everything from that, and it'll be unobtrusive."

"No." He blinked at her, but Honey just laughed. "Do both. Seriously. They have the sticker to peel off, *but* the website stays in case they lose it or peel that off before giving it away."

"Great idea. Thanks."

"See you at five?"

As he yawned, Josh nodded. "I'll either be

bright-eyed or bushy-tailed. I will not be both."

While Honey sang her way through 80s pop hits for two hours, Josh apparently didn't sleep. He arrived with two minutes to spare with a prototype of his ornament, complete with a semi-removable sticker on the back. "I just stuck it to my hand a few times to test it out. What do you think?"

The door jangled, and Milton and Atticus stepped in. The bird chattered, but Milton wouldn't let it fly around the bakery. Honey had a solution for that. "Let's go to my office. He can fly in there."

With everyone seated and Atticus exploring the rather boring room, Milton began a presentation on his laptop that Honey had to admit was pretty impressive. "Before we get to signs, I want to point out a couple of things. First. Joshua…"

Josh's head snapped up. "Yes?"

"Great work on the ornament."

"Some of it was Honey's idea—where I deviated from yours."

After giving Honey a thumbs-up, Milton said. "Okay, this promotion the town is doing…"

Her heart sank. He didn't like it.

"It's a terrific idea and at least a month late." With a few swipes of his finger, Milton showed how it should have started as "grateful for our customers" and moved into the "our gift to you" program it was meant to be. "The day after Thanksgiving that should have rolled out. So, you have a lot of background to make up. Honey might manage." He shot Josh an apologetic shrug. "I don't know if you can."

"Right."

"But that's all right. This is a long-haul process, and you've proven to me that you'll do the work so…" He pulled out an envelope. "Before I left, the last business I worked with gave me half of what's in there to give to someone else needing help. When Mercedes heard about your store and how hard you've been working, she took up a collection from other store owners and they sent that. So there's our budget to keep you going through February. We have to use it wisely."

Josh took the envelope, counted, relief and resistance growing on his features with every flick of his finger. Without saying a word, he passed it to her. Instead, he stared at his hands.

Come on. Say thank you or—oh. You're praying. Duh. Honey counted in half the time it had taken him. "A thousand dollars? That'll get him… what?"

"Inventory for one thing. We need to spend half of it on inventory. He's ignoring a huge profit source. But we're here to talk signs. I just didn't want Joshua to think that this promotion would be his ticket to success. It probably won't. This is why we're focusing mostly on other areas."

Every bit of Honey ached to say, "Well, that's just great, but I need a sign." Last night's lesson managed to curb that temptation. Barely. *Selfish. You're just being selfish.* Another part of her argued, *But I can't ignore what my business needs just because someone else's needs more.*

"Because we need to do this cheap, I'm suggesting two sign options. First…" Here Josh sat up and pulled out a small notebook and pencil. He opened it, ready to take notes. Just in case she needed to as well, Honey pulled up the notes app on her phone, rethought that, and called up her voice recorder. "Mind if I record this so I don't have to take notes?"

With that, Josh put away his notebook and took out his phone, too. "It'd be easier for me. Got coffee going yet, Honey? I'll buy."

"No one's buying anything." She hopped up. "I got so excited, I forgot to bring in breakfast. Hang on."

Atticus tried to escape when she left, so when she returned, Honey kicked the door with her foot and waited for Milton to capture him. Josh took the drink carrier and apologized. "Need me to get plates or…?"

"Would you? And forks? Behind the counter. I'll slice this baby."

Before she'd taken her first bite, Milton swiped. "First, I propose we paint this on your chimney. That thing is right there in front of your store, so you might as well use it to your advantage. I estimate about fifty dollars maximum. Less if folks have paint they'll donate."

It would be effective. "Hart of Noel" had been written vertically down the length of the chimney. A large painted book below it had "BOOKS" written inside with "and Gifts" below that.

"I like it!"

Josh pointed to the "and gifts" and asked, "What's with that?"

"We'll talk about it later, but that's your moneymaker."

Without giving Josh a chance to argue—smart man, she decided—Milton swiped the screen again and showed a large sign sitting at the edge of the property. It had been angled, and painted on it… a double ended arrow. On the right, the sign read,

"Books and gifts to feed your soul." The left side read, "Sweets to feed your cravings."

"I'm not sure that's what we should write on the sign, but I like the general idea of having a double ended arrow that connects the businesses and a theme for both businesses to connect them in customers' minds."

"But that's a lot of money to spend on something for just a couple of weeks."

Honey dropped her fork on her plate and stared. A quick shake of Milton's head just in time kept her from blurting out what she thought of *that* selfish comment. *Is he for real?*

Milton took a bite of his quiche, complimented her on it, and turned back to Josh as if he hadn't just ignored that outburst. "You're going to need to work with Honey on this long after Christmas. Books and coffee go together. Donuts and books go together. Readers get snacky. Folks don't like to sit around and just eat a donut or a cinnamon roll. They like to feel productive. So, they'll either be on their phones, or you can try to sell them a book. Ideally," he continued as if he'd just had a new thought. "Your store would be next to hers or vice versa. But across the street is close enough. And really, you guys might consider each having a small turnstile rack in your establishments. A book rack for Honey, a cookie basket or rack for you."

For the longest moment, Honey feared Josh would say no. She couldn't *make* him put that sign there, but she sure needed him to. *Oh. Right. Lord... I should have been praying. I am now. Help!*

It might be short, but she'd have to trust it was effectual.

Half a minute later, Josh finally nodded. "I see it. Yeah. I see it. Good idea." He looked over at her. "Are you all right with that?"

"I *love* it." Her internal critic winced. *Tone it down before he decides it's a bad idea with all that enthusiasm behind it.*

But to her, and it looked like Milton's, amazement, Josh just grinned. He shot a look at Milton. "You never doubt where Honey stands on anything. She lives life intensely."

That sounds like a compliment to me, but is it? He smiled…

"Not enough people appreciate that in others." Milton winked at Honey. "And not enough people appreciate that some people need time to ponder, consider, and evaluate before they have a good grasp on their best course of action."

Ouch.

"So…" Milton speared another bite of his quiche with one hand while fumbling in his pocket with the other. He spread out a few seeds on the table and tapped it to catch Atticus' attention. "Who do we know that can help us figure out how to build that sign on a worn-through shoestring?"

This time, Honey and Josh grinned at each other and said in unison, "Edgar Boyles."

After a lunch from the fusion food truck that Joshua hadn't been able to afford in months, they stood in his bookstore with the counter separating them. Milton pulled out a piece of paper and slid it across to him. Just the sight of that list set his stomach churning. He'd faced his greatest fears with less trepidation. Less than ten seconds after handing it over, Milton took it back, studied it, folded the paper, and tore off the top. "Okay, we're starting here."

It didn't solve everything, but five things to focus on instead of twenty did give him breathing space. "Gifts? This is a bookstore. Why are we doing gifts again?"

"Have you been to a brick-and-mortar bookstore lately? A third of that store is going to be stationery, bags, stuffed animals, T-shirts, bookish kitschy stuff."

Still skeptical, Joshua pushed back again. "But I don't have room for that stuff. I thought people were supposed to find their niche and stick to it."

After explaining the difference between writing and retail, Milton said, "People like to buy book friends things, but sometimes they don't know what book that friend would want. That's where this comes in. You can't do a third of your store, but we can definitely maximize space and add enough that even Honey could come in and find the perfect thing for you if she got your name in a gift exchange."

And speak of the "devil," Honey burst in the door. "Hey, did Edgar get back to you? What can I do to help get this sign up and doing its job? Oh, and you know what I was thinking?"

Both men just stared at her for a second, but Milton seemed to find his voice when Joshua couldn't imagine what the woman's crazy brain had done now. "No... but I'd like to hear it."

"The Hart of Noel sign. On the chimney. I

think you should wait until spring for that. I think the paint will go on better if you wait until then. Why do something now that you might have to redo later? We'll have the yard sign, and you do have the little one there."

"Makes sense," Milton said. He turned to Joshua. "What do you think? Will the paint cure better if we wait? She's right, the yard sign would suffice for a while, and this would save work and money."

Joshua, on the other hand, thought something quite different. He gripped the paper until it crumpled and tried to steady himself. "I think we know where Honey's priorities lie. Doesn't matter what happens to that book thing over there. Just make sure you get something that benefits me done." He faced her, jaw set, teeth clenched. Through those teeth, he ground out, "Unbelievable."

Honey's eyes flashed and her cheeks turned bright pink. "Unbelievable is right. I came over and offered to *help*. That's not all about me. That's about—"

"Offered to help get the sign pointing to *your* store up. First, it's your stupid behemoth blocking the sight of my store. Then when we find a way to make it visible, you just push that aside because hey, there's something in this other idea for me!"

"You're a jerk, Josh Hart. I was trying to save you time and *money*. That commodity you don't have much of, remember? But no. This turns back into how Honey Potts is only concerned with herself. You make me sick." She jerked open the door and then pointed to where Parnassus sat batting at Atticus' carrier. "And you should save that poor bird from your mangy old cat."

The whole store rattled and shook as the door slammed behind her. Joshua huffed and shooed Parnassus off the counter. "Why did I have to get paired with her? She's going to make a hard job even worse."

Milton said nothing. That churning in his gut returned. A glance at Milton showed the man watching him. He knew better, but Joshua asked the question anyway. "What?"

"Last night... the lesson. What part of that verse hit you hardest?"

His throat tightened as did his fist The list was now a ball of wadded ideas. "Um... 'is not easily provoked.'" Eyes closed, he whispered, "I just provoked, didn't I?"

"Yes..."

His eyelids flew open, and Joshua stared at Milton. "What?"

"I just wouldn't have chosen that one."

Well, we know which one Honey is. 'Does not seek its own.' It's not self-serving. Too bad she didn't listen. Then again, maybe he hadn't. He'd lost his temper with her again. And Joshua wasn't known for being hot headed. *Just with her.*

"Do you want to ask, or should I just tell you?"

"Let me have it."

Instead of saying what he thought, Milton repeated the verse. "Love 'does not act unbecomingly; it does not seek its own, is not provoked, does not take into account a wrong suffered.'" Joshua's confusion must have shown because Milton added, "Or as some translations put it, 'does not keep a record of wrongs.'"

Ugh. That hit him in the gut. "You think…?"

Milton nodded. "I think Honey feels badly for not understanding about the parking place. So, when she found a way to try to make it up to you, she was excited to tell you about it. But when she came over here to share and to see how she could help get *your* sign up, all she heard was her actions through your filter of how you see her."

"Ouch."

"Let me hit you one more time and I'll let it go." Milton waited for his nod and added, "I think right now, Honey feels like you only see her as the sum of her past mistakes. Who of us would want that?"

Before he could justify himself out of it, Joshua shoved the paper at Milton and took off across the street. The cold air hinted of more snow and bit through his flannel shirt. Once inside the bakery, he looked over at Emma Kroner and said, "Is she in her office?"

Emma just scowled.

It was the last thing he wanted to say in front of his neighbors, but Joshua forced himself to keep going. "I owe her an apology. Can I go back?"

"As long as you make it. She's crying."

Oh, great.

The office door was closed, and Joshua heard the sounds of sniffling behind it. The aroma of coffee and cinnamon should never mingle with tears. He knocked.

"Emma, just give me a few, all right?"

Joshua tried the knob and found it turned. He stepped in quickly and shut the door. Honey didn't even look up from her head buried in her arms. "Emma!"

"I'm sorry, Honey."

Her head flew up. Red-rimmed eyes, a runny nose. Never had Honey looked so awful. It tugged at a place in his heart that he'd left abandoned for far too long. "I—"

Unsure how she'd take his apology, Joshua leaned against the door, shoved his fists in his jeans and tried to smile. "You were trying to help, and I lashed out at you over my own insecurities. I hope you'll forgive me."

A hint of a smile formed. "Bet that was hard to say."

"You've got no idea."

"Oh…" she said. "I think I do. And I gave you reason to think I'd be all about me on this. I—"

"No!" At her startled look, the tears that filled her eyes again, Joshua shot his hands in the air in a move he hoped looked like surrender. "Sorry. I just don't think you have anything to apologize for. I just really hope you'll forgive me."

Honey pushed her chair back and stood. She stared at him for the longest time before dropping her gaze to the floor. "I hate this part of being a Christian," she whispered.

"What part?"

Still not looking at him, she folded her arms over her chest and sighed. "This whole forgiveness thing—needing to ask for it. Needing to give it. Having to confront all this stuff. I just want everyone to get along and stop needing the stuff to begin with. Isn't that what we got saved from?"

"So… what you're saying is that's a yes?"

That got him a glare and then a laugh. "Yes. I forgive you. If you'll forgive me." She winced before

72

adding. "If I'm honest with myself, I probably had some hopes for the sign benefiting me, too. But I wasn't conscious of it! I promise."

"Can I hug you?" He blinked at his own words. *Where'd that come from?*

Her arms flew around him. "That's the part of Christianity I love."

Only when Honey started to step back did Joshua realize he hadn't actually returned the hug. He wrapped her in his arms and held her—much longer than any hug he'd ever given anyone at church. Much longer than most hugs he'd ever given anyone—ever. *Did I just turn a 'holy hug' into something more?*

Seven

Fifteen days until Christmas and only fourteen of them shopping days. Milton stood in the middle of Hart of Noel and surveyed the changes. The counter—gone. They'd replaced it with a mini kitchen island he'd had found at a thrift store in Joplin. They'd also tucked it away in the corner to make the best use of the room's real estate.

A business in Rogers had a going-out-of-business sale on fixtures that they offered on the Facebook marketplace, so Milton went to get a turnstile rack and came home with two. The result was that most of the "looking forward to reading" books had been sent to the bakery.

The "gift" side of things was still coming along, but Milton had managed to get a large box of ornaments that he could pick up from a company in Siloam Springs. With all those put in place, he now took pictures both of the product for the website, and of the store for the Facebook groups and Instagram.

Charm. The little building had it in spades. The

problem was that while everything about Hart of Noel oozed the sort of charm that drew people in and made them want to stay, it wasn't as effective as the store in California had been. The tiny footprint—about the size of a modest kitchen—and the biggest part of the shopping season over, it didn't bode well for a profitable Christmas season.

I'll just have to get to work on the New Year stuff right away.

"Looks like a different place."

Milton turned and smiled at the man standing in the doorway. "Welcome to Hart of Noel."

"You the new owner?"

You must not be from around here, or you'd know I'm not. Milton stepped out of the way as he shook his head. "No, I'm just visiting."

"Heard someone took over the store. Hard to imagine Josh Hart even considering selling out. Had to come see for myself."

"He'll be back in a minute. He had to go ship a couple of packages."

Now that felt good to say. Joshua's first two orders had come in the previous night. Apparently, the big websites had run out of stock on a few of the new releases Joshua had ordered, and only little retailers with online shipping options were able to fill them in time for Christmas.

The burly man in blue and black buffalo plaid flicked the cuffs of T-shirt sleeves and rattled a few ornaments on their hooks. "Looks like a lot of junk to me." Before Milton could ask if he could be of assistance, even if that was showing the man to the door, the so-called customer stopped in front of the promotional display. "What's Jole-bocka-flod?"

Though he knew it was a waste of time, Milton explained the Icelandic "Christmas book flood" and the connection with Honey Potts' Bakery. "We have suggestions here for anyone on a shopping list." Milton deliberately left out "your." Starting with the top row, he pointed out each one. "The outdoorsman, the romance reader, the reluctant kid—"

"What's that one about?"

"It's a graphic novel—lots of pictures to help tell the story in fewer words."

"Comic book."

As much as he knew it would probably be a waste of time, Milton couldn't let that go. "Not quite. A comic book is like a weekly TV episode. A graphic novel is like either the entire series or at least the whole season in one book—except that it goes deeper into the characters' lives and things. They're really very different, but they appeal to similar reader groups."

That's where the man surprised him. "Gotta nephew what struggles with reading. His mama thinks he's got the dyslexia, but the tests say no."

For a man who sounded uneducated, this fellow obviously knew what he was talking about, and he cared about this nephew. "Some kids just aren't interested, so they don't put in the effort. Other times, the tests don't serve them well and there really is a problem."

"Think this would interest a kid of eleven? Likes video games with the funky faces like this?"

He had to be careful with that one. "Well, I can say that if I needed a gift for a boy who didn't enjoy reading but did enjoy manga or anime video games, this is exactly the kind of gift I'd want to try. Most likely, he'd buy or receive whatever games interested him, but he'd probably never pick up the book. Being given it… there's a chance."

"I'll take it." The man pointed at the historical Christian romance on the third shelf. "Got another one like that? I know my sister has that one. Saw it at her place the other night."

That caught Milton's attention. As he began wrapping up the book, he asked what the sister's name was. Hearing, "Becky Boyles, Milton nodded. "I know which one she wants next. She bought that one from Joshua." He pointed to the small section of Christian fiction. "Top shelf… um… third from the left. Yes. That one."

Before he could wrap that book, Joshua came in with a handful of mail and a panicked look on his face. Seeing the man there only intensified that panic. "Hey there, Peter. Come in to see the changes?"

"Becky made me. Said you needed the support."

And I owe you for a fine example of Mark Twain's, "Truth is the most valuable thing we have. Let us economize it."

For all the man's complaining, Peter left seventy-five dollars poorer, half his Christmas shopping done, and with several vouchers for Honey's cookies. Charitable or not, Milton couldn't help but wonder if the promise of those cookies hadn't loosened the purse strings more than anything else.

Once they'd passed out three ornaments to Honey's customers and sold another book, Milton shooed Parnassus into the tiny back room and allowed Atticus a quick fly around the shop. That relaxed Joshua just enough. "Want to tell me what has you looking all panicked?"

No, he did not want to talk about anything. He wanted to bury himself in a book of poetry and ignore life. However, *Sonnets of the Portuguese* was his current read, and love poems sounded like torture. Whatever had possessed him to think now was the time to tackle those?

As Milton put Atticus back in his carrier and let in Parnassus, he said, "I'm going to guess Honey."

"You sold her the book. You should know."

If he hadn't been confident that Milton would not lie to him, Joshua wouldn't have believed Milton's, "I sold her nothing."

"She's reading *Letters from a Stoic.*"

Laughter reverberated off the walls. Parnassus poked his head out from beneath the table holding a display of books by local authors and stared. Joshua didn't see what was so funny. "Care to enlighten me this time?"

"And you're panicked, why?"

"She'll hate it! Why is she reading a book on philosophy from ancient times? What is she thinking?"

Parnassus stalked across the room and plopped his backside on the floor beside Joshua's feet as if to say, "Yeah. What?"

As if they weren't having a discussion, and Joshua weren't having a total mental breakdown that he couldn't explain, Milton began hunting down other book options for the *Jolebokaflod* shelf. The answer came as he rearranged a few things. "I'd say that she's thinking that her project partner likes reading philosophy."

"So...?" Joshua stared at the man who clearly thought he was an idiot. "She's a cookbooks and probably cheesy romance kind of gal. She's not going to like Seneca!"

Milton turned to face him, another manga title in hand. "Sincere affection causes men—or in this case, a woman—to do what they do not enjoy in order to please someone they do."

"Chesterton?"

He shook his head. "Coleridge—Milton. Go rescue that poor girl."

But Joshua just stood there, hands jammed into pockets, cat at his feet, miserable. "She annoys me. She's too perky. If she'd never worn that stupid dress—"

"You would have found something else attractive about her." When Joshua would have protested, Milton added, "It's no use. I won't even bother to try to make you see it, but you're half in love with Honey. You're just not ready to admit interest, much less affection or more."

That protest burst from Joshua faster than ever—fast enough to make even him wonder if this wasn't one of those "doth protest too much" moments. "Occasional attraction brought on by good fashion sense is not tantamount to love." He pulled out his phone. "I'm going to give her a cookbook. She'd read that."

Just as he realized it himself, Milton said, "You'll need to order it, then. You don't have any."

80

A moment later, Milton laughed.

"What?"

"I just remembered something Harriet Van Horne once wrote."

He'd never heard of the woman, so Joshua asked, "Who's that? What book?"

"Columnist. She said, '"Cooking is like love. It should be entered into with abandon or not at all.' Maybe you should avoid cookbooks."

That did it. Joshua pulled out his phone, leaned against the new counter, and began scrolling the offerings from "the world's biggest marketplace." Thousands of cookbooks came up, so he filtered by publication date. That only took him to page ten to get the most recent releases. Several Christmas baking books, one general baking book… no. She knew her baking. She needed something that incorporated story with cuisine… something to tempt her palate for longer, richer stories.

One captured his attention. *Screen Doors and Sweet Tea: Recipes and Tales from a Southern Cook.* That would be interesting. Right next to it, *Faith, Food, & Family: authentic Mexican recipes and an en-couraging word.* That encouraging word sounded promising, too. "I'll get the one with the least number of pages."

Faith, Food, & Family won hands down. At half the size and a quarter of the pages, no way would Honey feel overwhelmed by the contents. Joshua shoved the phone at Milton. "What do you think about that?"

"I think it makes me hungry. I'm thinking about going to get something from that place down the street. Want anything?"

He wanted everything on the menu, but his

budget said he could afford the Ramen and scrambled egg he'd brought. "I'm good, but thanks. Oh," Joshua added as he remembered something. "Mom wanted to make sure I invited you to Christmas with us. Parnassus is staying home, and Buford doesn't have the oomph to do much more than take trips out back to do his business and chow down on the treats Mom overfeeds him, so Atticus could come, too."

The smile Milton gave him told a story all in its own. Wasn't there some saying about how behind every smile people hid a story? It sounded like part Shakespeare, part Austen, part Twain. Milton would probably know who said it, but Joshua didn't ask. He just waited.

Without hurry, Milton slid one book into the shelf and pulled another one out to show face-forward. He retrieved a mug from another shelf and set it next to a book about a bookstore. The mug read: Coffee + Books = Bliss. Appropriate. Then he pulled a slim volume off the shelf of Christian fiction and handed it to Joshua.

"You really should stop Honey from reading that book. Now. I recommend you give her that one while you wait for the other to arrive. Pique her curiosity and tell her it's just to tide her over until the one you think she'll like most arrives. Trust me, she'll read it."

Pulling on his coat, Milton picked up his bird carrier and headed out into what looked like a coming snowfall. Joshua ought to know. His knee had been given weatherman status after the "tiny skirmish" in the "sandbox" that had blown it out and earned him a medical discharge.

Joshua turned over the book in his hand. *Dear Self: twelve short stories of faith, friendship, and love.* "Oh, boy…"

Parnassus hopped up onto the counter and stared at it. After a head-rub of approval, he went yowling at the door, anxious for his midday treat. "Should I do it, Parney? What if she thinks I'm trying to hint… something?"

It happened once or twice a month—always at random. As if eschewing baked goods and loaded coffees for one day would counterbalance the caloric excess the rest of the month, a significant number of the residents of Noel and the surrounding areas abandoned the bakery in favor of whatever they ate and drank on those mornings. As usual, that left enough leftover baked goods to fill the Blessings Box.

So, as Emma popped muffin after donut after fritter after cinnamon roll into baggies for the fridge—they'd put them in the box on Sunday—Honey sat in her office with the world's most boring book. Sat might be an over-exaggeration. She half-lay, half-draped herself across the table-desk, head propped in hand. Sort of. It kept dropping to the book at random intervals, if truth be told.

Why… why… how can he read this stuff?

A knock didn't even perk her up. Instead, Honey moaned, "Emma, you can lock up and go home. Put the 'We'll be back tomorrow. Will you?' sign up. Oh, and take home what you want."

"Actually, I came to trade."

83

That did it. Honey drew herself up and tried to look remotely interested in the book before her. "Hey, Josh! What're you doing here?"

"Bringing a 'while you wait' gift for a gift that's coming."

"You bought me a gift?" Should she be concerned? Trojan horse, perhaps? Then what he said registered. "Wait, you brought me a gift for while I wait for a gift you bought? That makes no sense."

"It does to me." He pulled up a chair and reached for *Letters of a Stoic*.

Honey resisted. "Hey, I'm reading this!"

"You're still on the introduction."

"Well, you know how those things are. Dry as Ezekiel's bones, but it'll get better." *I hope.*

Josh was already shaking his head. "You'll hate it, Honey."

No, what she hated was how much she liked the way he said her name. This wasn't supposed to be a thing. The guy had made it clear that he would tolerate her—protect her, even—but friendship wasn't in his plans. Too bad. Those eyes... that beard... that mellow voice. She could see herself falling for a guy like him if he weren't so antagonistic to her. Then again... he was improving. A hair. Okay, so maybe a frog's hair, but a hair, nonetheless.

"You read it." The words blurted out before she could consider how they'd sound. Upon reflection, they didn't sound as desperate as she'd feared.

"I like philosophy. Seneca. Marcus Aurelius. Plato. Socrates—"

"Enough! Please. I'm trying here, okay?"

He sat facing her. If he'd gotten any closer, their knees would touch. Honey tried not to think of what

84

a shame it was that he hadn't. Dangerous territory.

Josh tugged the book from under her arm. "Trade?" He pushed a book over to her. The cover looked like antique stationery with an elegant, almost Victorian label framed in gold swirls. In the "label," the title: *Dear Self: twelve short stories of faith, friendship, and love.*

Love? No way. He reads romance?

He tapped the cover, and Honey caught a hint of whatever soap he used. Foresty and minty combined. *Nice.*

"I haven't read this one, but the author is good. Bestselling and popular with Christian fiction readers. I thought short stories might be nice because if you didn't like one, the book wasn't wasted. You could just go with the next one." He sighed and leaned back as if he realized how close he'd gotten. "Except on the way over, I noticed something in the synopsis."

Honey flipped it over. "What's that?"

"I think the short stories are threaded together somehow. I think they still stand alone, but if you don't read one, the overarching story might lose some richness." Before she could tell him she'd read every word, Josh added, "But I have another book coming. I think you'll like it better. It feels right up your alley."

"Gonna tell me what it is?"

Just like in every romance movie she'd ever seen, their gazes locked. Josh swallowed hard but didn't look away. Her peripheral vision caught the movement and translated it for her. "I had planned to surprise you," he whispered.

A giggle escaped before she could decide if it would annoy him. "By telling me you bought it?"

"Putting it that way…" There he broke eye

85

contact and pulled out his phone. "That's coming. It'll be here next week, I think."

The cover looked interesting. Mexican food was a favorite, and a cookbook. That sparked a revelation. "If cookbooks count, then I own *tons* of books!"

"They count." Josh eyed the book she'd attempted to read and peered inside. "I'll return this to the library for you."

"Why do you care?" Honey toyed with the dust jacket on the book he'd brought, not quite willing to look at him for fear of what he'd say. *I can hear it now, "I am just trying to get people reading again."*

"Maybe because I'm beginning to care." Her head shot up in time to see his eyes grow wide and dismay mask his face. "I didn't mean—" He jumped up. "I have to go."

A slow smile formed as he bolted from the room. "Well now…"

Eight

Crunching through the snow might not be everyone's favorite way to spend a morning, but Joshua loved the sound of boots in snow, and the fact that his cat refused to be carried but also hated slogging through it made for an amusing walk. However, as he neared the back entrance to his store, a sound sent despair spraying over him. Joshua knew that sound. Water. The pipes had burst. *God, really?*

Joshua raced for the back door, fumbling with his keys in his haste. Once he had it open, his feet sloshed through the water that now surged out the door unchecked. Parnassus jumped onto the crate by the back door and refused to move, but Joshua didn't have time to deal with the finicky cat. Three steps into the store, Joshua realized he needed to turn the water off at the main. He just didn't have a wrench.

With the yowling Parnassus in his arms, Joshua took off for home. Then a new thought came to him. Dropping the cat into the snow, never a good way to keep a feline happy, he backtracked, racing across the street to the bakery. Once again, half of Noel had decided to have their morning Honey fix and blocked most of the space in the doorway. Joshua pushed his way through the throng of hungry customers to the front and caught Honey's attention.

"Do you have a wrench I can borrow? I've got a burst pipe—water everywhere."

Honey slammed the cup she held down on the counter, sloshing the coffee everywhere, and raced out of sight. A few people murmured their sympathies. People in Noel were used to old buildings with insufficient insulation and a habit of bursting pipes. Some called it the town's "charm." Joshua called it a pain in the neck, the backside, the pocketbook.

Honey dashed into the room wielding a crescent wrench and passed him on her way out the door. Joshua took off after her. "Honey, wait! I can do it. I just didn't want to have to go home to get mine."

"I've got this. You go save your books. I'll be in to help in a minute."

It wasn't the first time he'd been tempted to forget all reservations and just kiss the woman, but it was the first time he couldn't do it even though he'd finally admitted it. Unwilling to risk Honey's wrath, Joshua decided to be smart and listen. He unlocked the front door of the store and wished he had a push broom. Just as he reached for the first row of soggy books on the bottom of the *Jolebokaflod* shelf, Honey dashed into the room.

"Okay, where do I start?"

Joshua started to send her for the push broom but asked instead, "Can you grab me one of the black trash bags in the storeroom on the shelf next to the back door? Actually, can you bring the whole box?"

"Sure! What else?"

"I—" But she was gone, and seconds later, he heard rummaging, grumping, and huffs of frustration. Finally, "Eureka!" told him she'd had success.

If he hadn't still been wearing his coat, Joshua would have been soaked by the time she brought him the trash bag, shaking it open as she approached. He dumped an armful of ruined books into the bag and his hopes for a successful future tumbled in after them. Even with the slight uptake in sales in the past week he'd never recover from this loss. A glance at Honey told him she knew it.

"Josh, I am so sorry. We'll fix this. I'll do whatever it takes. So now what?"

He had to get her out of there before he said or did something really stupid. "Do you have a push broom?" She didn't answer but the way she took off out the door, dropping the trash bag into the watery mass at his feet told him she must. Joshua grabbed the bag and began sweeping up everything that couldn't be saved and dumping it into it.

He'd cleared most shelves, and still no Honey. The cheap pressboard bookshelf that held his *Jolebokaflod* offerings listed to starboard as it began to sink in the puddle that pooled there. At least now he knew which way the floor slanted. Joshua grabbed every book on that shelf and stacked them by the register. He should have known anything with the word "flood" in it was doomed to failure.

As long as it was taking her, Joshua began to wonder if Honey had misplaced that push broom.

Then again, she had a bakery full of people who wanted their cinnamon rolls and wanted them now. Hey, who was he kidding? He'd be first in line if he didn't have a life's dream to chuck into black trash bags of death. *Melodramatic much?*

A rattling rumble reached him long before Honey came through the door. Joshua looked up to see her with a shop-vac in one hand and a push broom in the other behind her. Luke Armbruster from church carried two coffees and a box that could only hold one thing. Cinnamon rolls. *I think I'm in love.* "You are amazing."

Luke grinned as he handed over one of the coffee cups. "Well, Molly always says I am, but I'd say Honey—"

"All right, Luke, that's enough. We both know he meant me and I'm taking it." Honey winked. "A girl's got to take what she gets when she gets it."

Maybe he was crazy, especially with Luke standing there watching and taking in every bit of the exchange, but Joshua couldn't resist. "We'll have to talk about that later."

If he thought that either Luke or Honey would leave the supplies and take off to do their own things, well Joshua wouldn't have known his people very well. Honey, sure. She had a business to run. She didn't have time to help him shovel his dreams out the door. *Again, a little melodramatic.*

"Where's Parnassus? I haven't seen him. Is he all right?"

Guilt struck a pang in Joshua's heart. His poor friend. How could he have done that? Then again Parnassus had been rather finicky, so maybe they were even. "I may have tossed him in the snow when

90

I realized you might have a wrench. Forgivable offense under the circumstances?"

Luke's laughter rang out. "Well, I'd probably say so, but I doubt Parnassus agrees. Which one of us is going to go after him?"

"Which one," Honey shot Joshua a wink and a grin, "would Parnassus most likely come to?"

With everything off shelves that had been affected by the water, Joshua began sorting what he could save from what had to be tossed. He only half-listened to the exchange, but discovering his most expensive books had suffered just enough damage to make them unsellable, Joshua didn't join in. He picked up the collector's edition of the complete works of Narnia and removed the dust jacket. The water hadn't reached the actual pages, but it had damaged the bottoms of the covers, too. A picture book of dragons also ruined. The complete set of Wordsworth Classics Jane Austen novels, the ones he'd set there until he sold the paperback set on the top shelf and in direct defiance of Milton's suggestion? Also ruined.

A hand on his arm pulled him from his thoughts. Honey. Joshua looked over at her, ready to tell her to go on back to her own store—her own customers. But Honey shot him her killer smile and said, "We'll fix this. It's going to be okay."

"It won't be okay, Honey. I can't recover from this. It's too much. But thanks for trying."

Luke must've decided it was time to go find the cat, because he quit fiddling with the shop-vac and took off out the front door. Honey never took her eyes off him. "I mean it, Josh. We can fix this. That's a lot of books, I know. But we'll sell a lot more. And

I happen to know that there's this little thing called insurance."

"With a deductible that makes a claim not worth it. Seriously, they wouldn't pay a dime and I'd still not meet my deductible."

He'd known that meant he probably couldn't afford the store, but Joshua had been so certain he'd be able to adjust it before he ever needed to use it. He just hadn't counted on Old Man Winter taking against him. Or maybe Mother Nature was PMSing. Either way, he'd been dealt a blow that would easily be a couple of thousand dollars in losses.

"It's just a few books. It's not that many."

She didn't get it. Joshua draped an arm across her shoulders and steered her toward the door. "It's not just the books. It's the time lost selling what I need to sell to be able to have the stock I need to have to sell anything in January. It's paying rent on a building not bringing anything in. It's having to replace at least three bookshelves when I can barely afford to buy Parnassus Kitty Chow." He gave that shoulder a squeeze and pushed her gently out the front door. "Thanks for caring. I mean that."

"Josh…"

To drown out what he couldn't handle hearing, Joshua picked up the hose to the shop-vac and began sucking out water. *Can't afford to take you out to dinner, either. Can't really afford to make you anything but cheap spaghetti at home.*

Only once she'd gone inside her store did Joshua do what he knew he had to do. He called his supervisor at the chicken plant and asked to be put on full time as soon as an opening came up. The man said he'd be on the next week's schedule. As much as he wanted to take back the request, Joshua choked out, "Thanks, Tim."

Next, he started to call Milton but knew he'd crack if he tried to talk about it. Instead, he sent a text message.

Atticus rode along beside him as Milton drove through Jane, Missouri and into Arkansas. Bentonville, home of Walmart, was also home to a couple of interesting-looking bookstores. Reconnaissance was in order if he were to help Joshua keep his store afloat.

His phone pinged. Before he could tell his phone to read it to him, another came in. Siri read the first text message from Honey. "Hey, Milton? Are you coming in today? Joshua really needs some encouragement right now. His store is flooded. Pipes burst."

Milton's heart constricted.

"I'm scared. He sounds so fatalistic. He says he's out of business with this. That can't be true. Can it? What do we do? Call me if you can't come in today? Please?"

The next one was from Joshua. "Good morning, Milton and Atticus. I know you were planning on doing some bookstore hopping today. Well, I hope you haven't left yet. I appreciate all you've done for me, but 'Taps' is playing for the store. Everything on the bottom shelves is gone and a few where water trickled down the wall. Burst pipes. It'll take days to clean up this mess, and the Christmas spending will be almost over. I have to accept that I can't make this go. I'll find a way to get you the money your friends invested. Even if I have to borrow from my parents."

Another text message followed as Milton drove past a bleak-looking golf course.

"Oh, and I still hope you'll stay through Christmas. My parents are excited to have you."

A sign for Lankershire Boulevard said to take exit 98. He'd do that. Meanwhile, he called Honey. "Got yours and Joshua's texts. How bad is it, really?"

"I don't know!" He could hear her breathing heavy enough to be an old-fashioned crank caller. "I mean, There's probably twenty or thirty ruined books? The Christmas book flood shelf is ruined. He needs a new one there. Oh, and I have one at home he can have. Anyway…" She went on to recount every word Joshua had spoken and every impression she'd gotten.

"He's right. He can't have people in there until the floor dries out and the pipes get fixed." To someone else, she added, "Just put the leaves in the back of my truck. I'll store this in my guest room until we can bring it back."

"What's going on over there?"

"I moved out the big table. We usually just get school kids doing their homework on it, and school will be out in a few days."

Should he even ask what that meant?

"We'll put everything we can fit into that corner. I can keep his register behind my counter so that he doesn't have to take up space there, or we can run it for him. Either way. I think he's going to take more hours at the chicken plant if they've got room for him. They usually do."

By the time he got back on Highway 71, Milton had nearly forgotten the warnings about watching for speed traps. Were those along here or between Noel and Neosho? Lanagan, someone said. He hadn't seen a sign for Lanagan. Milton inched his speedometer up another three miles per hour. The back roads into Noel meant an average of forty miles per hour, so making up extra time now made sense.

"You're a good friend to him, Honey."

"He wants more… or rather," she amended, "he'd want more if he let himself. What's wrong with him? Or with me?"

Maybe it wasn't his business to butt in, but if Joshua really did give up, he might not have time to let things unfold without a nudge or two. "There's a line in what is generally considered the first modern romance. The man, after trying to convince himself that he doesn't love the woman says, 'In vain have I struggled. It will not do. My feelings will not be repressed.' I'd say that our friend has definitely struggled in vain. His feelings are resisting that repression, and he's at the precipice of the 'it will not do' portion. All that remains is for something to push him over the edge… and for someone to be there to catch him at the bottom."

"What happens in the book?"

Milton winced and took exit 5 for Highway H. "Well, in the book, he goes on to insult her and her family before asking her to marry him.

"She'd better have told him to get lost."

"She did." Milton discovered he was holding his breath and exhaled as quietly as possible.

"Good. So, no happily-ever-after? I thought

that was a romance law of some kind."

And this was why Milton Coleridge loved nearly all forms of fiction. Even people who didn't want to become interested inevitably did with the right inducement. "There is definitely a happily-ever-after. Eventually."

"What's the title?"

"*Pride and Prejudice.*"

Her groan told the story before she did. "That was one of the titles he had in the 'damaged but salvageable pile. Jane Austen, right? Like back in the pregnancy dress era?"

"Something like that."

Whether she ever heard that reply, he didn't know. The phone died as he entered one of the many dead zones around Noel.

Nine

Once he'd separated destroyed books from readable but not salable ones, Joshua shut down. Parnassus, who had ignored Atticus flitting about the store and remained stretched out on the counter as if determined to take up every inch of space possible, thereby removing all chance of using it in the cleanup effort, finally moved as he saw Joshua walk out the back door and down the road. It was a picture that belonged on a Christmas card—a guy and his cat walking through the snow. Well, it might have been if Parnassus had been sensible enough to be a dog.

One more man and two of the women from church arrived. Honey sent them across the street with arms full of books. "Just don't take more than you can carry without dropping. You drop it. You buy it."

"Hey, we're here to help!"

Melissa's protest fell on a heart of stone as far as Honey was concerned. "Yeah, and it's no help if Josh loses more money because we ruin the rest of his stuff."

"You know he hates being called Josh, don't you?"

She loved Melissa—really, she did. But that woman redefined know-it-all and took it to competitive levels. That, unfortunately, rattled Honey's cage and she acted without thinking. Again. Grabbing a sheet of paper from the printer with one hand, she dug out a Sharpie with the other. In seconds, she'd scrawled a huge 10 on the sheet and slapped it on top of the stack of books in Melissa's arms. "Give the girl a prize. She knows Josh best."

A gasp on the other side of the room snapped Honey back into reality, but not before Melissa sniffed and stormed off. Regret punched her down like dough in a bowl. "Ugh."

"Not right, Honey." That's all Luke said—all he needed to say.

Without another word, she rushed out, ready to bolt across the street, but instead, a line of cars coming in and going out across the bridge kept her stranded there in front of Josh's store for what seemed like hours. By the time she made it across the street, she opened the door of her bakery in time to hear Melissa say, "—thinks the sun comes up just to hear her crow."

"Don't look now, but I think you've just done one of them gender reassignment things. Never heard of a girl rooster before."

"You know what I mean! She just started orderin' me about like she'd been left in charge. Joshua Hart can't stand her. Everybody…" Melissa's voice trailed off into a whisper at the sight of Honey, but she finished, nonetheless. "…knows… that…"

Honey's plan to apologize tried to evaporate,

98

but a poke from what had to be the Holy Spirit prompted her to say, "Melissa, can I speak to you in my office, please?"

Without waiting for an answer, she led the way, but she didn't get out of the room before hearing Melissa add, "See what I mean? What is she, the principal now? We back in school or somethin'?"

Lord, come on! I came over to apologize, but come on. This is piling it on a bit much, don't you think? As if in reply only to her, the Lord whispered His instructions. *"If possible, so far as it depends on you, be at peace with all people."* Honey may have snapped back, *Fine*, but she'd never admit it.

Melissa stepped in the office, door open, and folded her arms over her chest. "What now?"

"I owe you an apology. What I said was rude, unkind, and… not okay." Oh, this was gonna hurt. "I hope you'll forgive me." *Why do we have to do that? It's awkward!*

"Fine. I forgive you. Just don't be so bossy. No one likes bossy. Do your own thing and leave the rest of us alone."

All Honey could think of was that old saying about pots and kettles. *Does she have a clue, Lord?* His reply came almost as an echo. *"…so far as it depends on you…"*

By the time Milton arrived, she had three of the bookcases installed in the corner of her bakery. She'd also sold ten books and had holds for five more piles since she hadn't had time to bring over Josh's credit card machine and register.

Milton set up Atticus' cage in the office and let the bird out of his carrier before heading across the street to survey the damage and make a plan. Left alone, Honey dragged Emma and Luke over to the back wall of the dining area. "Look, if we remove these two tables, we can fit more of Josh's stuff in here. What do you think?"

Emma said, "I think you should do it."

Luke shook his head. "I'd ask Josh, first. It *is* his store."

"It's just for a few days until we get his place up and going...." But even as she said it, Honey knew he was right. Josh didn't like being pushed out of his own decisions, and if she were honest with herself, she'd admit she wouldn't like it either.

"I'm going to his place. I'll be back. Luke, will you ask Milton what he'd put there if we did it? I'll call if he says yes."

With that, Honey took off up Main Street, past the railroad tracks, and down Sulphur nearly to Davis. His little pickup truck sat under a carport, which she hoped meant was his house. It was neat—tidy. Plain. Not a Christmas light around a window or down an eave. No wreath. Not even a Christmas doormat.

Because he's a guy, because he's a Scrooge, or because he's broke?

At her knock, a call came from somewhere, "Come on in, Ma. You didn't have to come."

Honey pushed open the door and was surprised to find a nice-looking living room set—couch, loveseat, recliner, coffee table. Large TV. *I thought you were broke.* The sight of a small but obviously good-quality dining table through the doorway told her he had good taste. *On credit, maybe? Is that why you're so broke?*

"Mom?" Parnassus dashed through the room and out of sight as Josh filled that dining doorway.

100

"Honey?"

Seeing Honey Potts standing in his living room might just put him over the edge. Joshua, ever gracious under pressure, asked, "What are you doing here?"

Did Honey seriously just snort? The mortified look that rearranged her features into something almost comical told him she had. "We were worried. We have questions only you can answer, but mostly…" She stepped a bit closer and slid one hand over the arm of his couch. "We just were concerned."

And by "we" do you mean "me"?

Another few steps brought her within just a couple of feet of him. Houses on this side of town were pretty tiny. Her hand raised, and for one irrational moment, he felt certain she'd slap him. Instead, she stepped a bit closer and laid it on his cheek with gentleness that shook him. Her thumb brushed at the corner of his eye.

Oh, no… they're still there. Joshua backed away, ready to flee into the kitchen, but she caught his sleeve.

"Don't… it's okay to hurt, you know."

"Honey—"

She shook her head and advanced, never shifting her gaze from his. "No. You're allowed to hurt. We're allowed to help. You might think this is over, but it's not. Right now, we have three of your bookcases in my store. I've sold books and have piles waiting."

"Pity sales won't—"

"Forget your stupid 'pity sales.' Almost every one of those people said something to the effect of, 'I kept meaning to stop, but I always had somewhere to go. I figured out that you can't always count on something being there tomorrow.'"

His coffee began brewing finally. The coffee pot he'd brought back home had begun to fritz—kicking on only when it decided to work. Apparently, that was now. "Coffee?" He winced. "It won't be as good as yours, but…"

"Sure." She followed him into the kitchen. "Nice table."

"If things keep up this way, I'll be selling it and everything else I own." He shot her a look. "I keep trying to convince myself to close the book on the shop, but I can't. I've planned this for years."

The tears that kept attacking him welled up again, so Joshua dug into a cupboard for mugs in a bid for self-control. "What do you like in your coffee?"

"Plain black works for me." He shot her a look. "No, really," she insisted. "I like coffee any way it comes."

They sat at his table just as he'd begun to picture the date he wanted to create and didn't have the guts to suggest. However, instead of the candles he'd planned to give his otherwise bland kitchen some ambiance, his Bible sat in the middle of the table and instead of plates of rather mediocre spaghetti, they each had their hand wrapped around cups of subpar coffee.

This will not work. It's a good thing I never let her see how she affected me.

"Why do you avoid me?"

Or maybe I was wrong about that.

"Don't try telling me you don't. You do. The potluck, at church, even in the post office half the time. I know you don't hate me—at least not anymore. I don't know now if you did—"

She'd ramble on indefinitely if he didn't stop her. "I never hated you. You irritated me, but I never hated you."

A smile played about her lips. "We have something in common. You've irritated me, too."

"Sorry."

Honey leaned forward as if to share a secret. "My dad said something last night when I admitted how irritating you'd been about the parking space."

And here I thought you'd been irritating about it. Apparently, she wanted him to ask. So he did. "What'd he say?"

"He said, 'Honey, when someone irritates you, it's usually because they care about you but don't know how to show it.'"

You have no idea.

"Josh?"

Will you ever finish saying my name? The answer to that seemed obvious enough. "Hmm?"

"You're never going to ask me out, are you?"

"I can't." At the protest she began, he reached over and took her hand. "No, really. I can't. I can ask you to have dinner with me, but it would have to be here. Cheap spaghetti. It's what I can afford right now. Not very enticing…"

She laced their fingers together and squeezed. "I like spaghetti." Before he could respond, she added, "And the company… totally enticing."

103

"Yeah?" It was a dumb response, but it's all he trusted himself to say.

"Yeah."

Maybe it wouldn't be so bad. Messy food, though. Maybe he could do a baked spaghetti dish with different pasta. One of those tubular things that fit on a fork. It could work.

"If you invite me, I'll bring the garlic bread."

"Friday—no, Saturday night?" He sighed. "I have to work Friday."

"Saturday night. I'll be here at six." She squeezed his hand again. "Can I bring dessert?"

Had anyone else asked at a time like that, he'd have felt like a charity case, but this was Honey. Sweet stuff was kind of her specialty. "Appreciate it."

"So, will you come down and see what we're doing? I need approval. I've already ticked off Melissa for getting snarky with her."

Well, I won't admit it, but she inspires that sometimes.
"Right?"

Joshua felt his face heat. "Did I say that aloud?"

"You didn't have to."

If his life had been a book, the author would have taken note of how empty his hand felt as she rose and urged him out the door. In that book, he'd have waited until they got onto the sidewalk and taken hers captive again. But this was the real life and times of Joshua Hart, not some silly romance novel. They walked back to the store with hands in pockets—their own pockets. Where they belonged. Those hands stayed warm, too.

Well, Joshua may have imagined what it would be like to hold hers all the way there. Perhaps. But he'd never admit it.

Ten

Saturday morning, almost eight o'clock. Joshua's blinker clicked with the precision of a metronome as he waited for the dozen cars ahead of him to pull out of the chicken plant parking lot. He'd have less than two hours to sleep before he had to be to the store. The overtime was a boon to his bank account and a killer to his health.

A horn blared, and Joshua, half asleep already, jerked his head up, peeled out onto Cliffside Drive, and shot over the bridge to Highway 90. A gray gloom hovered, promising a bit of snow if the temperature dropped enough. Once on 90, it was a quick drive to Main Street, over the bridge, past his store, and up to home. He barely made it to his carport before sleep threatened to leave him snoring in an idling truck.

Get out of here before some well-meaning neighbor decides you're trying to off yourself.

The shower he'd meant to wake him enough to get spaghetti sauce simmering in his Crock-pot only served to make him sleepier. He shot a text to his mother, asking her to come by and assemble it for him, set an alarm for nine-fifty, and collapsed on his bed.

Dreams of his childhood followed. His mother tucking him in and promising to make him soup so he'd feel better. His fluffy couch blanket cocooned him in blissful softness until Joshua became fully awake. *Why am I not sleepy? I should have a headache.* He peeled back an eyelid and stared at the clock. Two-thirteen. That didn't make sense. It might be overcast, but it was light out.

That's when the aroma of basil, garlic, oregano, and tomato reached him. Joshua flung back the blanket and raced through his house. "Mom!"

His mother had been there, all right, but she'd left—probably hours ago. Parnassus hopped up onto the table, clearly taking advantage of Joshua's panic. And it worked. He didn't even give the cat a scowl as he bolted through the house and into his bedroom. Jeans, Hart of Noel T-shirt, flannel shirt, socks, work boots—his good pair, of course. A glance in the mirror turned into a long attempt to tame hair that insisted on curling.

I really need a haircut. One curl hooked his ear like one of those cuff things his sister loved so much. *Today.*

With Parnassus under one arm, he jumped in the truck and ignored the cat's yowl of protest. "No time for a walk today." A glance at his phone as he slapped it on the holder prompted a groan. "Ugh. Ten shopping days left, if you count today, and I'm lollygagging in bed."

That stopped him right in the middle of Sulphur

Street. He didn't even put his truck in drive as he stared at Parnassus. "I just said lollygagging. I've lost my mind."

A punch to the gas shot him backward a few feet. Joshua slammed on the brakes, put the truck in the proper gear, and forced himself not to fly down the street at speeds designed to ensure either an accident or a ticket. For a nasty-looking day, the streets were full of cars. Even Harps old parking lot held a fair number of vehicles—including trucks with ribbons and crepe paper. Trailers. *The parade! I missed it!*

Joshua pulled his truck up behind Honey's Suburban and dashed from it, Parnassus on his heels.

"Hey, Joshua!" One of the women from church waved at him from across the street. Her two small children waved donuts at him and giggled at Parnassus racing down the sidewalk.

With a wave back, he took a detour into his store for a quick check on the curing paint. What he found stopped him short. Luke and a couple of the other men from the church were there, but instead of adding another coat of paint or screwing in bookshelf anchors, they were finishing up installing a wall of pine tongue-in-groove. The warm glow of the wood offered a cozy atmosphere to the store. Two of the shorter walls had been done already, and with just a few rows to go, this would be done in no time.

"What—?"

Luke looked down from the ladder before raising his eyes to the ceiling. "Lord, that woman…"

"What woman? Honey?"

Ben Grafton snickered. "We know where his mind is these days."

Ben, I remember when you were dating Rachel. You couldn't hear a door squeak without looking to see if she might possibly be stepping into your proximity. Don't even mess with me on this.

"Your *mother,* Joshua. She was supposed to keep you out of here."

"Haven't seen her." Joshua ran his hand along the pine by the side window. "It's amazing, but I can't afford this."

"My parents redid their cabin up by Branson," Ben said as he climbed down to grab another board. "There was almost enough left to do the whole store, but…" He jerked a thumb at the front wall. "We decided to leave that one plain since it has your slatwall on it already."

It would work. He could move all T-shirts to the one side and… *What am I thinking? I won't have the money to keep this place open.*

"You might want to get over to Honey's and relieve your mother. The town's been doing a brisk business with the after-parade shoppers. I actually heard some people from up by Carthage talking about how their friends mentioned the parade and craft show and decided to drive down for an afternoon of shopping and dinner over at the barbecue place."

"Hey, y'all. Thanks. Really. This—I'll be right back to help."

"No, you won't," Luke said in that tone that no kid who grew up at the Noel church of Christ would ever cross. "You'll send your mama home and help Honey where you can. We've still got a few hours before the snow's supposed to hit, so let's make the most of it. You have books to sell, and she's got folks to keep warm so they keep shoppin'."

Parnassus sat in front of the door, unwilling to budge. "Mind if he stays here? I can't bring him into Honey's, and there's too many people driving around for it to be safe for him out there."

"Leave him, but if he swipes my coffee off your counter, I'll dump what's left on him."

As if accepting that dare, Parnassus hopped up on the island and eyed the cup. Joshua rescued it in time and hooked it in the paint can holder on the ladder. "There. Safe from feline foibles."

If the look Parnassus shot him meant anything, he'd find an unwelcome package left in an unexpected spot soon. *Great.*

Getting in the door at Honey's proved nearly impossible. People packed the room at the counter, the tables, and even along the back wall where Hart of Noel made a credible showing despite the lack of space. His mother pointed out book after book on shelves that looked kind of sparse to him, and he wondered if he should retrieve some of the backup stock from home.

"You're doing well today." Joshua moved out of the way of an exiting customer as he looked around to find Milton. The man grinned from the table by the door. "I had to come sit over here to get out of the way. As soon as there's the slightest thinning out, I'm going to go over to the store and bring back a few more books."

"I have a couple of boxes at home—ones I didn't have room for with my first order."

"Great!" Milton nodded. "Your mom's a natural by the way. She's selling Honey out of cinnamon rolls like mad. Honey finally had to ask locals to redeem their cookies later this evening or next week because she's almost out. Right now, she's back there baking more cinnamon rolls!"

A glance over at his mother struck a pang to his heart. "Could you take over for Mom? I hate to ask, but she looks beat."

"I tried. She's... stubborn."

"Don't I know it." Joshua started forward and paused. "When I get her out of here, then could you? I know it's not your job, but just until I get back?"

Milton raised a coffee cup with its little bee sleeve and took a sip. "Ready when you are."

After a survey of the room, Joshua found a path that reminded him of an English garden maze but did the trick. He slipped up behind his mom and wrapped arms around her middle while squeezing her. "Thanks, Mom."

A book dropped to the floor with a bang that rang out in the room. "Joshua Hart, you scared me!"

"Sorry."

She laughed up at him and added, "Did you sleep well?"

"Too well. Missed the parade and left you doing my job." He kissed her cheek and turned her around. "Go home. Put your feet up. And thanks for the sauce. It smells great."

"I had a bit of Italian sausage left in the freezer, so I put it in there. Hope that was okay."

Joshua leaned close and whispered, "Is this smart? I mean, I am in no position to—"

His mom stood on tiptoe and whispered back, "Joshy... if you wait until you can afford to be in a relationship, you'll be single to the grave. Honey is a treasure. Don't bury her."

Frankly, he had no idea what that even meant aside from, "Stop dinking around and woo the woman." That much he translated well enough.

"Yes ma'am."

"That's my boy.

If Diane hadn't come in to help Emma, Honey would have been in a pickle, and pickles only taste good with donuts if you're pregnant—or so her mother insisted. *Lord, that's another thing to thank You for. Mom could have been craving pickles. Would I have been Dill? Sweet? Bread and butter? Maybe beets or okra? Yikes.* The reality hit her with the appeal of pickling brine. *Gherkin.*

The door creaked, but Honey didn't have the guts to ask how things were. The timer would go off in less than a minute, and she still had two more batches to twist and curl into the pan. Only when Emma didn't ask for something or volunteer information did Honey glance over her shoulder. All right, she'd finished twisting *and* the timer would go off in three... two... one...

"Josh! What are you doing there?"

"Watching the magic." He winked at her. The guy actually winked. "Half of Noel would kill for this view." At her huff, he winked again.

What's gotten into you?

The buzzer blared as she opened the oven to retrieve the baking cinnamon rolls and provide cover for her already burning cheeks. With them on the cooling trivets, she grabbed the next four pans of

111

cinnamon rolls one at a time and shoved them onto the racks. *Next investment, ovens that hold double what these do.*

He was beside her in an instant. "What can I do?"

"Tell me how things are going out there?"

"I got Mom to go home."

Honey gave him a smile. "She showed me a picture of you asleep." Should she do it? The red creeping up his neck answered that one. "Should've known you'd be one to sleep without a shirt."

That red covered his face. "Mom's dead."

With a wink and a snicker, Honey freed him from his misery. "You won't sell many bookstore-owner calendars with half a shoulder showing. Bookworms expect a whole arm at least. Maybe ask the guys over at the fire station how to do it."

Josh plunged his hand into a glove and shot her a glare. Maybe a mock glare? She'd just started to tell him he didn't have to help her when he stuck his finger in the frosting bowl and licked it off. "Mmmm... nothing better than Honey's..." Seconds ticked past as he gazed at her. "Sweets."

One hand fumbled about the table for her icing bag, while the other brushed damp tendrils off her forehead. She ripped off that glove and reached for another. "Where is that icing bag?"

Heart thudding, breath shallow, Honey blinked as Josh ripped off the soiled glove and pulled out another one, holding it open for her. Once properly gloved again, he pushed the bag into her hand and held it. "Save me a pan? I want to give it to Mom."

"Sure thing." Maybe it was time for a bit of flirting and ribbing all wrapped in one. "You know

112

that book you gave me?"

"Mmm…?"

"Not too bad. Sweet stories. Short and sweet, actually. And it made me figure out what is wrong with books."

If he stepped any closer, she'd be too unbalanced to hold that icing bag properly, but Honey wasn't about to move away, either. "What's that?"

Scooping up every bit of courage she had, Honey leaned one hip on the worktable and eyed him. "Romances are written by women. Men don't read them, so they don't know what kinds of things actually make women swoon."

"You think so, huh?"

Honey nodded. "Yep. I think if a guy wanted to *really* romance someone, he'd read them for lessons on how."

Oooh… I hope I didn't open a stink bomb there.

Eleven

His candlelit table might not have elegant tapers, but the little jars worked well, too. Thanks to Honey's challenge, a successful day at the bookstore, and almost two hours of overtime, a small bouquet of flowers from Harps sat in a jar with jute wrapped around the top, his mother's suggestion. At least it looked less tacky than the plain old jar.

He'd changed into a good shirt, washed his hair, and even blow dried it straight again. *Need that haircut.* He'd remind himself of that for the next week or two until he could make it up to Mom's for a buzz.

A salad in the fridge had plunged him into guilt. His mother shouldn't have to do the work of and pay for the elements of a decent date. Then again, if he could have one day like this every six weeks, he might just be able to make a go of the store *and* afford a decent date.

And I move back into my building tomorrow.

That shouldn't disappoint him as much as it did. Being forced into the same proximity as Honey all afternoon—well, it hadn't been torture. Or, rather, if

115

it had, he could stomach that sort of torture anytime. *When did she go from my archnemesis to someone who makes my palms sweat? Furthermore, why is that something I like?*

A knock jerked him out of his thoughts and into the present. He bolted for the front room and checked his shirt in the mirror. No spatters. Good. Another knock followed with Honey calling out, "My arms are falling off, Hart! Open up!"

I'm going to fall in love with a woman who bosses me around. I must be crazy.

Honey stepped into his house, arms loaded with canvas shopping bags. "Whew. It's cold tonight!"

"Let me take those. You can just hang your coat in the closet if you want. I'll be in the kitchen." He started to step back and decided to go for bold—probably broke too, but he'd consider it bold this time. Joshua planted a kiss in the general direction of her cheek and bolted for the kitchen.

You faced boot camp without blinking. Guarded against insurgents without once begging God to get you out of there. But you can't show someone how you feel? Freak.

The internal berating worked. By the time he'd gotten done informing himself of how pathetic he really was, Joshua was ready to go all out to show Honey there was more to him than a guy obsessed with parking spaces and selling books. *I can do this. I—*

That thought died at the sight of Honey entering his kitchen in that purple thing—tunic. That's what it was. His throat went dry.

"Okay, I recognize that look. You want to bolt. What'd I do now?"

Hurt. He heard it in every word, saw it in the way she hardened her features and tensed every muscle. He'd done that to her.

116

"It's not you." Joshua could have thrown the wooden spoon across the kitchen. *What, are you going to add, "It's me?" How original.*

"So, what's wrong with *you*, then?"

He had to tell her. "Confucius."

"Oh, this I've got to hear."

Here goes nothing. Joshua swirled spaghetti noodles into the boiling water and set the timer. "He said something like, 'Everything has beauty, but not everyone sees it.'" With more force than necessary, Joshua popped the lid on the pot. "I didn't see it, Honey. And then one day, I did. I—" How could he hope to explain what he didn't understand himself?

Honey pulled out a chair and plopped down. "I'm lost."

He grabbed the chair next to her and flipped it around. Straddling it, he draped his arms over the back and tried to meet her gaze—failed most of the time, but he tried. "You know how sometimes they put things behind curtains for a big reveal? They pull the cord, and the drapes swing back, and everyone finally gets to see the masterpiece?"

She nodded, looking a bit confused, but her lip twitched, too.

"Well… it's like you put on that green dress the night of the potluck and I saw you—really saw you for the first time."

"So…" She frowned. "Wait, you *liked my dress,* so you avoided me?"

This isn't going well. "Um… sort of. I convinced myself it was just attraction—I noticed you looking extra nice. You were still the annoying woman across the street as far as I could see. It made me even more determined to avoid you."

117

Water boiled over, and Joshua jumped up to deal with it. Honey snorted. "I don't believe this. You were ticked off that you liked my dress, so you—so what's this about tonight? Why am I here if I'm just that annoying chick across the street?"

Oh, boy. He licked his lips and checked the contents of the bag. Bread. He could heat the bread. As he cranked on the oven, he tried to explain. "That's the thing. You aren't. I—" How could he get her to understand before she took off on him. Not that he'd blame her, perhaps, but leaving now… He'd never get the courage to do this again.

Arms folded over her chest, now Honey just looked ticked—seriously furious. "Oh, really?"

"I—"

When he broke off again, Honey rose slowly and waved a hand at the bread he pulled from the bag. "Enjoy dinner. I'm going."

He caught up with her at the door. "Don't go. I don't blame you, but—"

"You don't want me here, Josh."

"But I do. I just—" He swallowed and tried again. And failed. Only the hope in Honey's eyes kept him fighting when the defeatist side of him demanded he give up. What had Milton said last night while they were finishing up the second coat of paint at the store?

"I'm sorry, Honey. Really. If I l-liked you less, maybe I could talk about it more."

The hand that had reached for the doorknob dropped. She watched him for a moment and giggled. "I'm such an idiot."

"Huh?"

"For a big reader, you're not very eloquent—

118

although that bit about liking me was pretty good."

Truth forced him to admit, "Not mine. Austen—modified a bit."

One moment she'd been ready to storm out of his house, her coat still hanging in the closet. The next, she stepped into his arms and slid hers about his neck. With her gaze locked on his, she asked, "That was from the author who wrote the thing about feelings wouldn't be repressed? And then insults her while proposing?"

That sounded familiar. *Pride and Prejudice,* wasn't it? He'd read it in his list of classics. "I think so."

"I've been reading one of the books that got ruined. At least she got one scene right." While Joshua worked up the courage to ask if he could kiss her, she watched him. Then she was gone. "Come on. I'm hungry."

Guess I'll save that kiss for dessert?

Without Parnassus prowling the store, Atticus was allowed to flit about as he pleased while Milton and Joshua worked to reassemble the store before evening church services started. While he focused on the "profit junk," as Joshua insisted on calling it, Joshua focused on the small section of classics, bemoaning that more people didn't want those over *Journey to Her Heart.* "I wasn't excited about reading Dickens any more than the last guy, but *Our Mutual Friend* had great lessons on human nature."

Milton couldn't argue that, but a line from the book seemed apropos. "'No one who can read, ever looks at a book, even unopened on a shelf, like one who cannot.'"

"But people can read," Joshua argued. "They just *don't*. They want to scroll through their phones or blather on about stuff that has no meaning or purpose. You can quote Dickens' Mortimer all you want, but I prefer Descartes."

So engrossed was he in his work, Joshua didn't even notice that Honey had come in. *You would prefer a mathematician turned philosopher.* Milton gave her a smile and covered his lips with his finger and asked the expected question. It would have been cruel not to. "And what did Descartes say about reading that resonates with you?"

"'The reading of all good books is like conversation with the finest people of the past centuries.' If we're going to talk all the time, shouldn't we converse with people who have proven themselves to have basic common sense?"

Honey began searching for something in her phone. A glance at him pleaded for him to keep the conversation going. After squishing the little Christmas tree's branches up just a bit more to make room for a stack of journals, Milton came up with an appropriate response. He needed something to temper Joshua's book woes. "Perhaps that is what inspired E. B. White when he said, 'Books are people—people who have managed to stay alive by hiding between the covers of a book.'"

"I'd say…" Honey's opening prompted Joshua to start, drop the book he held, and take a few steps to greet her. She continued, reading from the phone as if determined to get it right. "'Give him a book and he'll read all day.'"

"Not if you're around."

Look at him put his heart on the line even in front of me.

The quandary of how to ask about the previous evening's date dissipated in Honey's kiss to his cheek, in Joshua's gaze. *I should have known you'd be private about your relationship—in all respects. I wonder how that's going to work with Honey's "lay-it-on-the-table" approach to pretty much everything...*

"Isn't he adorable? And to think I thought he was a jerk."

"I was."

The look Joshua gave her told Milton this slow burn of a romance was about to burst into roaring flames anytime now. *I just hope I'm here to see it.* They didn't need him—not now. He had a few things to go over with Joshua, but the man wouldn't be capable of keeping his mind focused on business now that she'd arrived.

The door opened again, and a woman peered around the corner. "Are you open? I saw people inside, cars out front, but the sign said closed— Oh! Look at that!" She went straight for the new (thanks to Honey) *Jolebokaflod* shelf with its large sign plastered across the front and a smaller definition below it. "My daughter was telling me about that. Finland stays up all night on Christmas night and reads or something like that."

Iceland... and it's Christmas Eve, but you have the general gist, anyway.

"I can help you, sure. Come on in. We're just getting ready to reopen after a flood of our own." Joshua gave her a meaningful look. "The pipes burst this week."

"Oh, wow. We're just on our way home from Neosho, and my cousin said I had to stop and see the town—said there were a lot of changes, and she wasn't kidding! A *bookstore* in Noel. That's wonderful." She snatched up two books. "I'll take these. My daughter will be so impressed that I remembered it."

He would have liked to have stayed and watched Honey's amazement at the way Joshua went from reticent "suitor" to book enthusiast in the space of just a few seconds, but he'd need to take Atticus back to their trailer, have a sandwich, and clean up before church. The moment he pulled out the baggie of tiny apple chunks, Atticus flew to the carrier and settled inside to munch.

"See you at church," he whispered as he left.

The drive back to River Ranch brought on a touch of what the old books would have called "the melancholy." Christmas was ten days away. After that, he had a government contractor job in Birmingham, one that would take him a good six months to do if the preliminary reports were even close to accurate. Maybe he'd find a bookstore there. Find a way to save another one from closing. Find another couple to watch—maybe help, even—fall in love.

Find someone right for me?

But he'd leave Noel before he saw the end of Joshua and Honey's story. "That's the beautiful thing about romance, Atticus."

The bird chattered between bites, and Milton liked to think he'd asked, "What's that?"

"Only in salvation and romance is the end the real beginning."

122

Twelve

December 23rd

One more shopping day until Christmas. For the last ten days, Milton had made him promise not to look at the books. *"I'm keeping them updated. I promise. You focus on building your store's reputation and preparing people to need you in the new year. That's it. That's all you need to do right now,"* he'd said.

But tonight was the night. "The reckoning," as he'd begun to think of it. Milton probably already waited in his house for him, but Honey had promised to come, too. However, she had an enormous order for the assisted living home in Anderson, and the cars picking up the order had just left. With the day's deposit and receipts in hand, Joshua dashed across the street, wincing as he came down wrong on his leg.

The next step nearly made it buckle. The next brought searing pain. *Need my brace.* He'd learned the hard way. At the first sign of pain, he needed KT tape, ice, heat, ice again, and his brace. In that order. Then once swelling went down, he needed to do all his physical therapy exercises until the pain and resulting stiffness were gone. Still, Joshua didn't allow himself to complain. Some gave their lives or minds in service to their country. Joshua gave his knee. *A small price to pay for the privilege of living in this country.*

He found her scrubbing down the stainless-steel worktable in the middle of the kitchen. "Hey, Josh! I'm almost—what's wrong?"

Didn't know it showed. The fine line between toughing it out and lying nudged his conscience. "Knee's bothering me." Well, that was the truth, anyway. That's when he realized she'd see him nursing it and opted for full disclosure. "I wrenched it on the rough patch out there."

"Oh! Didn't—isn't that—do you need ice?"

Ice. She had heaping gobs of it, as opposed to the two ice trays in his ancient fridge. "Yeah, actually. Can we fill a few bags of it? That would save me having to run to Harps."

In seconds, he had a stool to prop himself on and she had several large polybags laid out. One by one she stuffed two inside another one and filled it with ice. Those she shoved inside a double-black trash bag and went for her office. "I'll get my truck and be over here in just a minute."

"You don't have—"

"Don't argue with me, Hart!"

Do you realize you reduce me to just "Hart" when you're affectionately annoyed?

Joshua did manage to stop her from carrying the bag of ice bags all the way to her Suburban. "Just set them outside the door and grab them when you come back for me," he said as he hobbled—the pain was becoming impossible to ignore now—to the front of her store.

That earned him a squeeze of his hand and a, "Be right back."

Left alone, he checked out the corner that still held a small selection of his merchandise. From across the room, it looked a little sparse, but had he paid attention to how it looked from here before he'd left the last time? He didn't think so. Still, the ornaments were definitely fewer in number. No doubt there. At five and six dollars apiece, it wouldn't pay the light bill, but it did seem to add up.

"Sell those all year round," Milton had told him. *"People will want souvenirs from 'The Christmas City' even in August."*

Honey pulled her Suburban parallel to the store and rushed to throw the ice bags in the back seat. Meanwhile, he hobbled to the step, winced, and started down. Honey nearly bit his head off for not waiting for her, and he might have argued, but having an arm around him and her close… *When a guy feels like an idiot for wrenching an old injury, it's a balm.*

She flipped a U-turn right there in the middle of Main Street and shot past the Harps parking lot. "Wait—my truck."

"We'll come get it after you've had some ice and maybe something to eat. Bet you're hungry." She shot him a look as they neared the railroad tracks. "Where's Parnassus?"

His forehead beaded with perspiration. "Uh, oh."

In less time than it should have taken, she turned left at the old Boston Realty building, made a three-point turn and shot back down Main Street before he could stop her, and all without him feeling like he'd been thrown against the side of a rollercoaster. *Talent...*

The last thing Honey Potts needed was a cat with a Napoleon complex. Tail swishing, much too close to the small nutcracker ornament next to a picture book of the iconic Christmas ballet for her comfort, Parnassus studied her. He flicked it harder. Honey dove for and barely caught the thing before it toppled.

"Really Parny?"

The cat growled.

"Since when do cats growl? You really do have small dog complex." Honey tisked and added, "I thought you were above canine nonsense. You're a cat for heaven's sake. Act like it."

Parnassus rose, stretched, and shot out a paw. The business card holder went flying—as did all the cards. The score was tied.

Honey lost patience. "Josh is out there in the truck hurting. He needs ice and a bit of pampering, if you must know. Now knock off your tantrum and come on."

Though he didn't leap into her arms, even Honey wasn't optimistic enough to expect that, the tail flicked a little less wickedly. His eyes bored into her. She could almost hear his thoughts. *He left me here for* you. *What did you expect?*

Feeling very much like the new girlfriend that the guy's kid feels will take away his daddy, Honey inched forward, hand out and hoping it worked with cats as well as dogs. "He'd have come to get you himself. He's a good guy, remember? He's just in pain. You know… like when that brute of an animal attacked you way back. Remember that? Remember how Josh took you in and got you fixed up?"

The tail stopped flicking at least.

Honey took another step closer. "He probably eats Ramen twice as often as is reasonable just to keep you in cat food. He doesn't deserve this. If you won't come for me, come for Josh."

After a slow blink, Parnassus jumped down, gave her a withering glare, and stalked to the door. He plopped his backside down and twitched his tail again as if the feline equivalent to toe tapping.

"If you were a girl, I'd say you had a diva complex." As she opened the door, the cat nipped at her ankle and shot out. "Parnassus!"

At the same time, Josh opened the truck door and called for the cat. The animal halted his dash down Main Street, turned, and flew into the truck as if it had been the plan all along. When Honey slid into the driver's seat, he growled.

"I think we have a jealous cat who doesn't want to share his human with the girlfriend."

Her face flamed. *Did I seriously just call myself the girlfriend? Out loud?*

An arm slid across the back of the bench seat and his hand rested on her shoulder. "He'll have to deal."

I could get used to this.

Milton had Atticus tucked away in Josh's spare room, so Parnassus had the run of the rest of the house. Of course, the only room he wanted was the one he couldn't have, but Honey didn't have time for fur-baby histrionics. She had to prop Josh's leg with a pillow, to apply ice to that knee, to set a timer, and to retrieve a heating pad. All while keeping one ear out for Milton's verdict.

It sounded pretty good. Sales were even better than in the summer during what would probably be Josh's busiest season aside from Christmas. She started to congratulate Josh when Milton said, "But it's not enough. You won't make it on this. You'll burn out if your cash doesn't first. You can't keep working nights and days. So, I have a few options to help get you through."

The defeated look on Josh's face stirred her to action. Honey plopped herself down on the floor next to Josh and looked up at him. "We've got this." To Milton, she added, "What options?"

The plan unfolded. Wednesday through Saturday—store open with half days on Wednesdays and Thursdays. "Then you have an online side business—editing for authors, fact checking for authors, writing book descriptions, doing virtual assistant work, tutoring kids, teaching history or philosophy to private school students…"

That gave Honey an idea. "What about teaching 'Get It Right' classes for military stuff. Everyone's always saying the books and movies get it wrong. He could teach writers how to get it right—or is that w-r-i-t-e? Hey!" Honey winked at him. "That could be your secondary business name."

"This all sounds great. I'd probably like most of it—except the editing stuff. Not my bailiwick. But…" She felt the sigh he didn't release. "Milton, I can't quit my job. I only have the rent paid for this place through April. I need—"

"Got that covered." Milton explained the six-month plan—building up those other businesses while still working at the chicken plant until he could make it. "And you sock away every penny you make in the interim for September and October. Those will still be lean months unless we can boost the online stuff. Oh, and you can write articles for websites. They pay peanuts, but your blog posts are popular with the people who read them. We'll boost your visibility there, too. Anyway…"

And off he went again. Finally, he pulled out all the numbers, including what Josh had handed over when they arrived. "This is where we're at." He hesitated. "Not to be offensive, Honey, but I need to make sure Joshua is comfortable with you seeing this. It's pretty sensitive."

"Go ahead. I'll probably need her help over the next few months anyway, so she might as well see what she's getting into when I show up going, 'What do I do to save my store now?'"

Save the store… Why did that—? "Oh! I forgot!" Honey jumped up and retrieved her purse. From it, she pulled her contribution to the meeting. "I've been talking to all the churches around here. What we don't have in tourists, we make up for in churches, eh?" She waved it at the men. "I talked to all of these, and they said they'd buy their Bible study books and things through Josh—with a few stipulations, unfortunately."

"Such as…?" Milton asked what Josh obviously wanted to but looked afraid to.

129

"The Pentecostal church said as long as we didn't sell porn or satanic—occult he said, I think—books, they'd support us. The Baptist church said they'd do it only if we agreed to carry a few Bibles. Luke agreed as long as we didn't skip church to do inventory, but I think that was a joke…"

After the few qualifiers had been shared, Josh shook his head. "I'll carry Bibles. Sure. One of each version or something. I'll never sell occult books, but that doesn't mean someone else won't think I do if they see Narnia or *The Lord of the Rings* trilogy. I'm not going to play that game."

"Good." Honey and Josh stared at Milton. The man now sat with Parnassus purring on his lap. "Doing what you can to accommodate is one thing. Jumping through hoops like a trained seal is another. I think we've got it." Milton rose and set Parnassus aside. "I'll try to return in June to see how it's going—do a reset if we need it. You have my number and my email." He gave Josh a stern look that even made Honey squirm. "Call or email the second something looks like it's going downhill. Stopping that snowball before it gets up speed is better than trying to create a block halfway down the hill."

Whatever that meant. Josh seemed to know, though. He started to rise, but Milton ordered him back into his comfy spot. For a little guy, he sure could be commanding when he wanted. "I'll let myself out."

"Still coming to Mom's on Thursday?"

At Milton's nod, Honey added, "Church tomorrow night? We're doing a ham with all the fixings." She gave Josh a wink. "See, I'm almost there. If I learn to drop my Gs, I'll sound like a local!"

"Not hardly," Josh added. "But you sound just fine the way you are."

Maybe it was cheating, but Honey didn't care. She walked Atticus and Milton out to his Land Rover and leaned against the driver's door. "What are his chances of making it?"

"If he's willing to be creative, he can do it. This town really is supportive, and if he starts the book clubs I suggested and has readings on Saturdays for the kids… it's likely he'll do just fine. If he gets lazy or stubborn about what he thinks a bookstore should be, though…"

"I've got it. He won't. And I'll call you way too much at first. Hope that's okay."

"It's great. I want him to succeed. He's just what this town needs, and…" Milton gave her a smile that would steal some woman's heart someday—might have stolen hers if she hadn't handed it over, lock, stock and barrel, to Josh. "Why do we use gun terms to mean 'completely,' anyway?"

"Well… there's nothing more complete than a gun ready to fire so…" Milton reached around her and opened the door. "Atticus is getting cold… and so is Joshua. As I was going to say, you're what he needs. Go do what you do best—give him some of that wonderful Honey Potts optimism."

Honey rushed in, eager to help with swapping out heating pad for ice, offering him a drink, resting her head on his chest with one arm thrown around him—that must have been awkward, but he wasn't

131

complaining. "He's more confident than you think, Josh. He's just not giving you a rah-rah-everything's-okay rally. We're going to have to work that."

We. She said that before. "What do we need to do?" Or something like that. It's like she's invested now, and she's not even a reader.

"Josh?"

He allowed himself the privilege of running his hand through her hair. Her eyes closed, and Joshua reveled in a moment he would never have imagined wanting. *She likes it—likes me. Best Christmas ever.* "I love that you're so invested in a business that means nothing to you."

That jerked her out of her—or his, rather—comfy spot. She sat bolt upright and scowled at him. "This business means everything to me now. It showed me the real *you*! I may not be a huge reader... yet. But if you're half the salesman you need to be, you'll convert me."

"One cheesy romance at a time?"

A slow smile formed. "You know how I got through that book you brought me?"

He had no clue. He'd tried reading the sample online and while well written, it wasn't his thing.

"I imagine the hero and heroine—why do they have to make the female equivalent sound like a drug, anyway?"

As heady as he felt with her so close, it sounded about right to him. "Hmm..."

She laughed and leaned close. "You know... I always thought you were handsome, but seriously, Josh. Those eyes..."

Was it his imagination, or had her gaze dropped to his lips for a moment? Joshua took a peek himself and nearly lost his head. *I cannot—*

"You want to kiss me. So do it before I ruin things and do it myself."

You'll never wonder where you stand with her. That has to be a good thing.

For the record, a first kiss while lying on a couch with his knee propped in the air ranked as one of the most awkward moments in Joshua's life. He missed her lips the first time, fell back as his elbow slipped off the couch the second time, but whoever said the third time is the charm… Had he been prescient or something?

That kiss began with the awkward hesitancy that characterized the whole of Joshua's romantic experience and culminated in a glorious punctuation mark. Honey dropped her head back to his chest and said, "Joshua Hart, you'd better fall in love with me and fast, or I'm going to beat you to it."

Epilogue

He hadn't enjoyed an old-fashioned Christmas in… well, Milton didn't want to think about how long. Joshua hadn't exaggerated when he said Buford wouldn't bother Atticus. No, that ornery bird had made a nest of Buford's shaggy ruff and spent half the morning snoozing with the dog. Milton zipped photo after photo to his friends in California, marveling at the ridiculousness of a bird and his dog.

With the Potts doing Christmas on Saturday so Honey's sister could be there with her family, she spent the afternoon at the Harts' house as well. Best Christmas present Milton could have asked for—seeing Joshua slowly becoming more comfortable in her presence. *He's probably fine when they're alone now. Wonder how long it'll take him to put an arm around her when someone might see.*

Children dashed through the living room now and then, one of them always stopping to stroke Atticus on the head before shooting off again. Most of the time, however, they spent in the basement where, according to Joshua's sister, "Kids belong. It's the twenty-first century version of kids being neither seen nor heard."

But just as the late "dinner" preparations drew to a close, Joshua's father called everyone into the living room. Milton stood off to one side, a part of the scene but not, and watched as the man pulled out a battered Bible that looked as if it had been through life's battles. In a voice that showed where Joshua had inherited his, Mr. Hart began reading. "'Now in those days a decree went out from Caesar Augustus, that a census be taken of all the inhabited earth….'"

When was the last time he'd "sat in a family circle" to hear the Christmas story read? *Too long, Milton. Maybe it's time to think about putting down roots again.*

Milton shrugged off that thought. He'd consider it later. Now was the time for swaddling clothes, mangers, and "glory to God in the highest."

A girl of about nine snuggled up to Joshua, tears forming as she listened. Joshua held her close, pressed his cheek against her hair, and whispered things no one else could hear. But his eyes remained riveted on Honey seated next to his mother.

Just who are you really holding, Joshua Hart?

The hush that fell as Mr. Hart closed the Bible lasted for just a few seconds before chaos erupted. Laughter, "dibs" on drumsticks and the wishbone, calls for what had happened to the salt and pepper shakers, and teasing. Heaping gobs of teasing.

Atticus grew antsy, so Milton put a few seeds and a couple of pieces of bell pepper in the carrier before seating himself near Mrs. Hart and offering to pass the rolls Honey had brought. Folks like the Harts did that to you—made you feel like you were part of the family even when they had every reason to assume they'd never see you again.

Could I be that person if I had a home? Would I know how to make someone feel that welcome—that comfortable?

After dinner, a ballgame came on in the family room. Games appeared on the dining table, and Milton decided it was his time to go. Protests followed him out the door, but Milton needed to be on the road as much as they needed time to get used to what their family would look like soon enough.

Mrs. Hart hugged him and thanked him. She pressed a small wad of money into his hands and whispered, "For the next person. Do something like this for someone else. Please."

Milton shoved it in his pocket without looking at it and promised. Mr. Hart shook his hand and assured him he was welcome to visit anytime. "You can pull your trailer right up there in the yard and hook it up."

"I'll remember that. Thank you."

Once the engine was running and Atticus had been installed on his perch, the children gathered around the Land Rover for a minute before dashing off to continue some dance-off game in the basement. Honey and Joshua alone waited with him. The men shook hands, and Joshua choked up. "I don't know how to thank you."

His own throat constricting, Milton just shook his head and tried to steady himself. "You gave me a wonderful holiday. I haven't had so much fun in months. Thank you."

Honey, however, threw her arms around him and squeezed until he couldn't breathe. "Thank you," she whispered. "Forget the store. Thank you for Josh. I know you were a big part of him opening up. I—"

The first tears hit his neck before she pulled herself away and wrapped her arms around Joshua, shoulders shaking. Joshua smiled, shook his head, and patted her back with the awkwardness of men the world over—the ones who have no idea how to comfort a woman.

Behind the wheel, Milton waved, put the Rover in gear, and pulled away from the house. In the rearview mirror he saw Joshua look down at Honey, brush hair from her face, and kiss her until they became a black blob in the darkening sky. *Needed that, Lord. Thanks.*

His chest still tight with emotion, Milton turned to Atticus. "Birmingham or bust, eh?"

The bird chattered and preened as they rolled around the curves and past the bridge to Main Street. This time, he'd head south down Highway 59. "That was a great Christmas though, wasn't it Atticus? Nice nest there you had in Buford's hair."

Atticus didn't respond. The little towns passed one by one as Christmas in the Ozarks drew to a slow close. Something Chesterton had written once came to mind. "You know, Atticus. I think what he said was true. 'Christmas is built upon a beautiful and intentional paradox; that the birth of the homeless should be celebrated in every home.'"

Author's Note

Our family is a bit obsessed with ornaments. It all began when my mother bought the first Hallmark ornaments the year I got married. After that, every year she bought each of our kids an ornament until it became too expensive. I mean, we had a lot of kids. So, I took over. On Black Friday, you'll usually hear Bing Crosby singing (or maybe Frank Sinatra… or Michael Bublé) in the background as my kids (almost all adults now) start decorating the tree. "Hey, here's your baby's first Christmas."

"Has anyone seen Nolan's other train?"

"The Salvation Army won't play again…"

Hours later, while the family sleeps, I sit back with all the lights off and gaze at the wonder of a tree of memories.

Tree day kicks off our Christmas celebration, but almost as beloved is whatever day one or more of the kids decide it's time for "Grandma's sugar cookies." My mother-in-law has the BEST recipe ever. It doesn't actually use granulated sugar at all—powdered sugar is the secret ingredient. That and almond extract. Mmm… The cookies aren't too sweet that way, and you can add sugar sprinkles or frosting without making them taste like a sugar factory. They still have *flavor*. Imagine that. These are the cookies Honey made and gave away to Joshua's customers. They're also the cookies that may have just saved his store.

Here's the recipe!

Lorene's Sugar Cookies

Ingredients

- 3 cups powdered sugar

- 2 cups butter softened

- 2 tsp vanilla

- 1 tsp almond extract

- 2 eggs

- 5 cups flour

- 2 tsp baking soda

- 2 tsp cream of tartar

Directions

In a large bowl, beat the powdered sugar, butter, vanilla, almond extract and eggs with a mixer on slow to medium speed, or do it the old-fashioned way and use a fork. In another bowl, mix the flour, baking soda and cream of tartar. Combine bowls until well blended. Cover and refrigerate for 2-3 hours. It works REALLY well to roll out your dough now between layers of parchment paper. It cools much faster. Just sayin'.

Preheat oven to 375°F. VERY lightly grease your cookie sheet or use parchment paper. Divide dough in half. On a lightly floured surface, roll each half about 1/8 inch thick. Cut with cookie cutters and decorate with colored sugar now if you don't want frosting. Try not to overwork the dough. Let the dough chill again if it gets too warm from rolling and rerolling.

Bake for 5 to 7 minutes or until edges are light brown. Remove from the cookie sheet. We like to flip upside down on newspaper or parchment paper to trap in the steam. Makes them extra amazing. Allow to cool completely before decorating further.

Note:

I took a few liberties with Noel, Missouri. First of all, when I began writing this book, the building where Hart of Noel sits was empty. By the time I was almost done, Sammy's Scoops, an ice cream parlor, had been installed. That's when I learned about the pine tongue-in-groove walls, so I added it for reasons of my own. Once upon a time, there was a bakery almost directly across the street, but now that bakery is up on the other side of the railroad tracks. I left it where it is for story purposes. The Blessings Box is a thing. People leave boxed food, produce from their gardens, baked goods, and even shoes and clothes there. For Christmas, one of my mother's friends is wrapping MANY sets of twenty-five books for kids to pick up and have a book a day to read for Christmas.

There is no Noel Revitalization Project, and the town really is struggling. But Noel pride is strong and fierce, and I can totally see them embracing something like this someday.

Acknowledgments

Seriously, this book could not have happened without several people in Noel, Missouri and of course, my mom. I cannot tell you how many times a day I went, "Wait… is that here… or there? Do they have this? Has there ever been a bookstore in Noel? What's the name of the street when you first come off the bridge?

For that I went to my mother first. Sometimes, however, it was the middle of the night, and I was afraid I'd forget to ask when she got up, so I'd send a message somewhere or another. I'd like to thank Bruce Arnold for answering my email to the Noel, Missouri website and for telling me about the Facebook group. I'd like to thank the helpful folks on the Facebook group for answering my questions when my searches came up dead for things like street names. For those who were irritated by me asking "the obvious," I assure you I tried before bugging anyone. Sorry to inconvenience you. Diana Henretty (the genius behind the Blessings Box) and Pam Lett (the wife of "Luke") were also right there with answers every time I had a question.

Noel? This book's for you. My heart has a very special "Noel-sized" place in it, and most of that place is filled with the lovely family at the Noel church of Christ. Miss you guys!

The Mosaic Collection

Pieces of Granite by Brenda S. Anderson
Watercolors by Lorna Seilstad
A Star Will Rise: A Mosaic Christmas Anthology II
Eye of the Storm by Janice L. Dick
Totally Booked: A Book Lover's Companion
Lifelines by Eleanor Bertin
The Third Grace by Deb Elkink
Crazy About Maisie by Janice L. Dick
Rebuilding Joy by Regina Rudd Merrick
Song of Grace: Stories to Amaze the Soul
Spines & Leaves by Chautona Havig
Written in Ink by Sara Davison
Open Circle by Stacy Monson

Learn more at
www.mosaiccollectionbooks.com/mosaic-books

Chantona's

Recommendations

New Cheltenham Shopkeepers Series
The Ghosts of New Cheltenham
Something Borrowed, Someone Blue
Ghosted at the Altar
The Bells of New Cheltenham
The Stars of New Cheltenham

Thank You!

I hope you enjoyed reading *Hart of Noel*, my unintended but hand-to-write-it book in the Bookstrings series. I'll be releasing the official first book, *Twice Sold Tales*, in 2022. If you did, please consider leaving a short review on Amazon, Goodreads, or BookBub. Positive reviews and word-of-mouth recommendations count because they both help me know what I've done well and what I need to improve as well as help other readers to find quality Christian fiction.

Thank you so much!

If you'd like to receive information on new releases and writing news, please subscribe to *Grace & Glory*, Mosaic's monthly newsletter at www.mosaiccollectionbooks.com/grace-glory/

If you'd like news about my books, the ones that go free, or new releases, sign up for my own newsletter at chautona.com/news.

Manufactured by Amazon.ca
Bolton, ON

35045425R00088